Baggage

Wendy Phillips

D1569313

Coteau Books

© Wendy Phillips, 2019

Edited by Alison Acheson
Designed by Tania Craan
Typeset by Susan Buck
Printed and bound in Canada

Library and Archives Canada Cataloguing in Publication

Phillips, Wendy, 1959-, author
        Baggage : a novel / Wendy Phillips.

Issued in print and electronic formats.
ISBN 978-1-55050-970-0 (softcover).--ISBN 978-1-55050-971-7 (PDF).--
ISBN 978-1-55050-972-4 (EPUB).--ISBN 978-1-55050-973-1 (Kindle)
        I. Title.

PS8631.H57B34 2019   jC813'.6   C2018-905774-2
                                                  C2018-905775-0
Library of Congress Control Number: 2018952788

2517 Victoria Avenue
Regina, Saskatchewan
Canada S4P 0T2
www.coteaubooks.com

Available in Canada from:
Publishers Group Canada
2440 Viking Way
Richmond, British Columbia
Canada V6V 1N2

10 9 8 7 6 5 4 3 2 1

Coteau Books gratefully acknowledges the financial support of its publishing program by: the Saskatchewan Arts Board, The Canada Council for the Arts, the Government of Saskatchewan through Creative Saskatchewan, the City of Regina. We further acknowledge the [financial] support of the Government of Canada. Nous reconnaissons l'appui [financier] du gouvernement du Canada.

To my father,
Archibald McEachern Phillips (1921 – 2014),
who brought up his children with the conviction
that a better world was just around the corner,
no matter what our previous baggage.

Part 1

Ms Nelson

The boy leans against the smooth stainless steel
of the baggage carousel
in International Arrivals,
scans the faces of travellers
his eyes wide
his forehead creased.

Behind him
wheeled Samsonites
backpacks
child seats in plastic bags
jostle down the conveyor belt.

I wait
beside my jetlagged students
in the Customs line,
watch him
from a distance.

Thin, brown,
alone
he looks like
baggage.

Thabo

The faces
of passengers
are all colours
but I do not see
the one I look for.

Travelling people
look past
reach around me
for their baggage.

A voice
through the speaker
calls out names of cities
Toronto
Los Angeles
Tokyo
and more things
I do not understand.

Languages
swirl around me
like birds

words
don't settle
fly away
through the hissing
glass doors.

Leah

The bat cracks
a ball soars
towards the field lights.

Over the ball field a plane roars
as it glides in for a landing
at the International Airport
the other end
of the city.

I watch the lights from centre field
wonder
if it's my sister coming home

or some other exotic
unconnected
strangers
arriving from the other end
of the earth.

A raindrop
hits my cheek
always a threat
in fall ball season.

I keep an eye
on the sky
wait for the fly ball
to drop into my glove.

Ms Nelson

Most parents have arrived
rushed past me
embraced offspring
pulled them
        jet-lagged,
        nostalgic,
        laden with souvenirs
        from their Japanese hosts
out to the parkade.

My eyes burn
from too many hours awake,
cheeks ache
from smiling
professionally.

With only one student left
I send my grateful colleagues home.
No need for us all to wait for stragglers
and I have no children
no husband
waiting for me.

October rain splashes down outside.
Dreariness swishes in
through automatic doors.

Brittany

Ms Nelson stands guard
under the airport's massive
art installation
      indigenous carvings,
      looming wooden
      First Nations welcome people.

My mother is late
again.

My phone buzzes
as I connect to the world.
I text my sister.

      Where are u?

She answers
      Mom's emerg shift ran late.
      traffic

#jet lag
#13 hours from Tokyo
#12 days away from home

That can wait.
Typical.

Thabo

I am still waiting
after three hours.

Before she left
the old woman told me,
"Wait here.
I will get food."
Her eyes looked everywhere
except at me.

She took my travel book
my papers,
smacked my head when I asked,
"Can I go with you?"

Now
I am still waiting.

I did what I was told.
      I don't know what else
      to do.

Ms Nelson

There's always one parent
tied up
forgetful.

This time it's Brittany's.
She fumes
tosses her hair.
I spy the Tim Hortons doughnut shop,
Canadian comfort food

tell her I'll be back.

Out of the corner of my eye
At the base of the Clayoquot welcome figures
I see the boy again.

In the shadow of the outstretched cedar arms
he hugs his knees
rocks back and forth.

Leah

Sweat
chills my skin.

My sister has arrived
from her international travels

needs her carriage.

Traffic jam at the airport
means Brit will be sitting
spitting
mad.

I close the car window,
long to pull off
my cleats
wash the home base dust
from my hair.

Mom grips the wheel
peers through the windshield.
She smells of antiseptic
latex-free gloves
sudden death

ER smells.

But this
being late
is her real emergency
today.

Brittany

Ms Nelson must be pissed
that she has to wait –
some legal thing.

She stops
in front of a black kid
who leans against the plexiglass wall
around the totem pole
bends over to hold out the bag

and I think

*She should watch
those honey crullers.*

The boy takes one
downs it,
looks at her with big dark eyes.

His clothes are light
for west coast October rain
but they look goȯd
on him.

I take a selfie
with the boy in the background
post it on Instagram.

#tired of waiting

Thabo

My body shakes.
I stay as still
as possible.
I don't know where she went,
the old grandmother who brought me
to this strange, cold place.
      Mme Moholo, o ea kae?

Faces around me
most as pale as salt
their voices sharp
and flat
and hard.

I don't know where
the real people are.

Ms Nelson

I'll get to the bottom of this.
This child should not be left alone.
Anyone could take advantage.

Thabo

The grandmother told me
RUN
if I saw police

but this woman
with the large white face
takes me to them.

I tell them,
      "Ha ke tsebe"
            I don't understand.
They shake their heads
look at each other.

One is Chinese,
the other wears a turban.

They look at me
I try to show nothing
that can make trouble.

Brittany

I thumb through texts
Courtney's student council info
Tricia's update on the coffeehouse talent show
Kevin's offer to pick me up.

I check likes & comments
on my Instagram
check Twitter & Snapchat.
I answer some
like
share
retweet
send sleepy emoticons
see my follower count is up since yesterday

look up from my phone.

Ms Nelson has the black kid by the hand
is marching him
towards the information desk.

Even after 13 hours in the air
ten days counting student heads
she still has that
take charge
no nonsense
walk.

I need to know
what's going on
get up
when she waves me over.

Leah

When we finally walk
through the automatic glass doors
into the warmth of Arrivals
Brittany isn't mad
like I expected.
She's head to head
with her teacher
who holds a slim, brown boy,
by the arm.

Brit's excited.
"He's been abandoned.
Who knows
what they intended?
He's just been left
at the airport
like unclaimed baggage."

When Mom says
sorry we're late,
Ms Nelson waves her apology away.

"This boy needs help.
It's a good thing I'm still here."

A Sikh man in a uniform
and turban
walks towards us.
His eyes are tired.
He walks like his feet hurt.

Mom hugs my sister,
waves at me to follow.
"Thanks, Ms Nelson.
We'll get this one home."

KEVIN

Her posts tell me
she should be home
by now.

I can't stop checking my cell
for a message

just for me.

My parents won't be home from work
for hours.
The house rings with silence.

I connect my iPhone to bluetooth speakers
crank up Arcade Fire
to chase it away.

I offered
to get out of badminton practice
pick her up at the airport
but she said
don't bother

as if it's a bother.

I check my phone.

Nothing.

Leah

Brittany hammers
on our bathroom door.
"Hurry up Leah."

Nice to see you too
big sister.

Downstairs at the kitchen table
Mom smiles.
Brit flows down the stairs
like a wave,
eyes dark
with dramatic hollows.

I settle into the back seat
of the family
as Brit opens her bag
pulls out shimmering silks
white-faced doll
wood sandals
little porcelain figures
of Hello Kitty.

Not much different
from the Daiso downtown
but they smell of foreign markets
Tokyo traffic
impossible sophistication.

She pulls me to my feet
wraps folds of cloth around me
pulls in my ribcage
with a stiff wide belt
pulls it tight until

I can't breathe.
"Isn't it great, Mom?"

In the mirror
I stare at my reflection,
the kimono gaping awkwardly
on my thin body.

I unwind everything.
"You show me."

The kimono lends Brittany
a curving, transcendent grace.
She flutters a painted fan
slides bare feet into sandals
pouts like a geisha
twists her hair into a bun
with a chopstick.
Irresistible.

Her years in Drama
have taught her
to slip into a personality
like putting on a coat.

I fiddle with my Winnie the Pooh phone charm.

Everyone in Japan
has one
Brittany tells me.

She's two years ahead of me
but I know
even when I'm her age

I'll never be like her.

Brittany

I tell them
about the boy at the airport.
Mom leans forward
her Japanese silk
rustling.

"No one knows
where he comes from
or his language.

"He's just a kid,
no family
all alone.

"Ms Nelson and I
got him to Immigration.
They said
they'd take care of him.

"He might be a refugee
a child soldier
maybe
a terrorist's kid
maybe
a victim of child trafficking."

I show them his pictures on my phone.
He could be a teen model
with his smooth, coffee-coloured skin

prominent bone structure
hollow cheeks
huge liquid brown eyes.

Ms Nelson wants me
to look up the process
of separated minor
refugee claimants.

Maybe she'll make him
a project
for bonus points.

KEVIN

First day back
she seems happy enough
to see me
but her public
absorbs her.

She wears some outfit
from the Asakusa market.
When I touch her shoulder
its silkiness
takes
away
my breath.

She flashes me a smile
turns back to the others.

"We need to take action,"
she tells the Leadership class.
"This kid has nobody, nothing.
He's defenceless."

Brittany loves projects
loves to talk to crowds.
She can persuade anyone
to join her.
Her favourite part
is getting people passionate
about issues
they've never heard of.

Not that there's anything wrong
with that.
It's easy
to see we should care about
homelessness in the Downtown East Side
AIDS in South Africa
mudslide victims in the Philippines.
The hard part
is what to do.

That's my job. She tells me,
"Just find something
we can donate to,
doesn't matter what.
I'll get the money flowing."

We're a team.
She does passionate crusader.
I do researcher sidekick.

Sometimes I wish
I was an issue

and she could get passionate
about me.

Brittany

English teacher drones on
about poetic devices.

I scribble slogans in my Writing Practice notebook.

> OPEN A DOOR TO A NEW LIFE!
> SUPPORT REFUGE FOR THE HELPLESS!

> SHINE BRIGHT LIKE A DIAMOND!
> SAVE THE WORLD ONE CHILD AT A TIME!

> HOW FAR WILL YOU WALK TO SAVE A REFUGEE?

They all sound pretty solid
Maybe a poster series
made into memes
Multiple shots, multiple slogans.

The boy is cute,
kind of exotic.
Leah can photoshop pix
add slogans
post on social media
print 11x17 posters
on the CADD lab colour printer.

A few sound bites
from Kevin's research
we'll be good to go.

I can hardly think
about anything else.
This is different from other campaigns
        collecting blankets
        or coats

24

or canned food
and sending them away.

Once we all went down
to the soup kitchen
served the homeless
but that was only one afternoon
and the people who came
were smelly old men
with swollen noses
and red eyes
sometimes families

no one who looked as good
as our kid.

Mrs Farr walks between desks
checking our metaphors.

I show her my writing.
The boy was a wilting tropical flower
shrivelling in the breath of the North Wind.

I know what she likes.
She moves along.

I'll go see Ms Nelson
after Kevin updates me
about the refugee thing.

I need to send Leah in
with a camera
to wherever he is.
She's got an eye.

I've almost got it
figured out.

KEVIN

Church youth group
starts with check-in
then discussion topic
then business.

The meetings can be lame
depending on who comes
but my mother gives me shit
if I miss it.
It's easier just to go.

Brittany came once
but said it was too
religious.

My check in
is about the airport kid
what might happen
how I'm trying to figure out
what we can do.

I don't mention
Brittany's project.

Tonight's topic is The Good Samaritan.
The Rev is excited,
swings his arms
in big circles
bushy hair waving.
We hear the original
(Good News Bible version)
and then he shows a news clip
on his iPad

air-played on the Apple TV big screen
about a small plane
that crashed onto the highway near the airport
drivers running over
pulling passengers
from the burning plane.

"Yeah," says Courtney.
"I remember, my cousin was caught in traffic
for, like, five hours
because they closed the bridge."

"One rescuer guy," says Salvador,
"got third degree burns,
didn't even notice."

"My sister's
brother-in-law's friend
was supposed to be
on that plane," says Tony,
"but he cancelled,
like, last minute."

We all discuss
where we were,
who was injured,
who died.

The Rev talks about
what it means
to do good,

why we should care about strangers
but most of us are caught up
in our own stories.

I think
he's disappointed.

I'm a little embarrassed
for him
when he wraps it up
with an obvious statement
about Living the Faith,
how Goodness is More than Words.

We listen politely
and move on
to plan the Christmas party for the Sunday School
our bowling night
in November.

Leah

I stay up late
finish my English essay
fiddle with my online computer science project.

Yoko, my dog,
lies on my feet,
eases the ache
from two hours of the punishing
catcher's crouch.
She snores quietly
soothingly.

On my sketch pad
I draw faces
of manga hero boys
with spiky dark hair
confident grins.

They look
just a little
like Kevin.

I rip them out
crumple them
throw them in recycling
before anyone can see.

KEVIN

Walking home
through dark streets
I think about the discussion.

It's easy to see the good
in rescuing people
from a burning plane crash.

But can you help everyone
and still keep your own life?

What if they take advantage?
Will you be the loser
who always says
YES?

The Rev wants us to get involved
gives sermons on
"Making a Difference"
"Being Someone."
He was a marcher
for something important
in the 80's.
But our congregation is hardly
revolutionary material.

At home
I finish my English essay on
moral choices in *The Crucible*
return to my research on child refugees in western countries.

The legal language is hard
but spits out words
trauma-slavery-stateless-detention-shackles-separated-minors-alone

My brain's too tired to understand
the article from *Refugee Law Journal*
but I see real problems
for this kid.

He doesn't need a Good Samaritan
to pull him from a burning plane.
He needs a lawyer
a "Designated Representative"
paperwork
a passport.

Brittany keeps telling me
how cute the African guy is
how much she wants
to save him

but it will take more
than good looks
and good deeds
to beat this bureaucracy.

I turn out the light.
A plane crash
is a lot simpler,
I think in the darkness.

Everyone can see
who's on fire.

The Reverend

I came to my vocation late.

Before I answered the call
the mountains were my cathedral
the wind through the poplars my call to worship
the clean air of autumn my priest's robe
a flock of migrating geese my choir.

      It wasn't enough
      for the girl I loved.
      Neither was I.

Here in the city
it's harder
to be uplifted
by the wonder
of a Higher Power.

Ms Nelson

Brittany hovers
at the classroom door
after the final bell.

I wipe the whiteboard
enter notes for Monday's lesson
on the War of 1812
close my marking folder.

She looks fresh, fired up.
I brace myself
for her enthusiasm.

> "So like Kevin said kids like this
> fall through the cracks
> and sometimes even go to jail."

At my blank look she rolls her eyes.

> "The boy from the airport.
> Did he get a foster home?
> How can we help him?"

I tell her he's in good hands
that the social worker was looking
for a placement.

Brittany's eyebrows rise,
her face wide-eyed
with what looks like innocence.

"Kevin said with no passport
no proof of age
he could end up in jail.
He said it's called 'stateless.'

"I would call but I don't know who
and they would tell you more
because you're a teacher
and they'll listen to you.

"Don't you think
he might need a lawyer
or better clothes?
He's not dressed for winter.

"Do they even have,
like, Walmarts in Africa
that sell warm jackets?"

I hold up my hands
to stem the flood,
tell her I'll call,
let her know Monday.

Brittany's face lights up
and I can't help but smile
with her.
She scribbles her number
on a lime-green post-it note.
        "Please, Ms N, would you text me?
        I'm so worried.
        If he needs a place

we've got an extra bedroom.
My mother said it would be okay.
And I won't share your number,
not with anybody."

As the door shuts
behind her
I shake my head.
She knows exactly
what she's doing.

My involvement was going to end
with reporting the boy to Immigration.
I had no intention
of getting in too deep.

We all want to do the right thing
but after last year's school trauma
with that boy from Central America,
        Miguel something,
it took months
to get back to normal.

In Brittany's eyes
I see a reflection
of my old passions.
She's longing to make
a better world.

Hard to resist.

Leah

For two weeks
while she was on her Japan exchange
I missed my sister
but I'm relieved
when the door shuts
and Brittany heads out to teach piano.

The intensity in the house subsides.
I can finally get my mother's attention.
"I'm going to Alisha's place
to work on our Socials project."
She nods.
"Call if you need a ride home."

Alisha lives around the corner,
along the river
across the wooden bridge
through the carefully tended park.

We live in a neighbourhood of heritage-style houses
with cottage roof-lines
and white picket fences.

It's a cleaned-up little fishing village
in the corner of the city
Only a few fish boats left now,
nothing smelly or dirty,
no more fights in the streets,
not so many fishermen lost at sea.

The fishing industry is mostly
in the museums now.
Tourists like it.

I kick aside brilliant fall leaves
cross the walkway by the fountains.

Brittany is teaching a piano lesson
in the condos nearby.
She has a student list of four
all little kids.
They love her
set out cookies and milk
when she comes to their houses
like she's Santa Claus.

I quit piano early
strum a guitar sometimes
alone in my room.
Performances make me nervous.

Sometimes I wish
we had another kid
in the family.
It would be nice to have
a sibling who looked up to me.

Alisha is at the door in sock feet.
"So what's up at your house?
Everyone's posting
that a cute African guy
is being thrown in jail
because he doesn't have a passport.
Everyone says
Brittany's going to save him."

She's disappointed
I have no updates.
My phone has been charging
on my bedside table since this morning.

I've missed all the online talk
but they trust Brittany
to do the right thing.

I promise Alisha
I'll tell her first
when I know anything.

Ms Nelson

When I get home from school
all I want
is the chair on my balcony
a glass of wine
the delicious promise of Friday afternoon.
Since the divorce
I've relished these moments alone.

But a worm of worry burrows in.
I have an hour
before government offices close.
I dig out my cell phone
ring the Ministry of Children and Family Services.

At last
I break through bureaucracy
to the social worker in charge.

Her voice is tired, tight.
She tells me
he's been put in detention.
No paperwork
no proof of age,
no nationality
the Department of Immigration
considers him at risk of flight.

> "It's Immigration Holding, not jail,
> but the boy is not at liberty."

Guilt swells.
I left him with professionals,
confident of the promise of care.

My anger shows.
The social worker's voice is weary.

> "No one knows
> whose jurisdiction it is.
> He says the woman he was travelling with
> took all his documents
> and disappeared.

> "It's hard to place his age, or nationality.
> Children from developing countries
> look younger than Canadians
> because of malnutrition.

> "They say
> he could be a man,
> not a boy."

My breath catches at the nonsense.

> "Just give me a number. I'll see about that."

Part 2

Thabo

Green walls close in
Doors lock

No one tells me
why I'm here
where I'm going
where the old woman went.

The other man in my room is older,
speaks a white language
not English.
He lies on the bed
stares at the ceiling.

I fall asleep
at strange times,
wake with bad dreams

fire
boots
fists

fear

that someone
will find out.

Brittany

Ms Nelson calls
as Dad and I do dishes.

Leah's at fall softball practice,
Mom's got a shift at the hospital.
It's frozen lasagna night.
Yoko gets the leftovers.

Ms Nelson wants to talk to Dad
and I have to hear it all
second hand
through Dad's confusion.

He rolls his eyes at me.
"She said her mother offered what?"

I rinse.

Dad hangs up in silence.
In his slump at the table
I read his yearning
for Mom.

> "We have the extra room, Dad.
> I'll take responsibility
> with the Global Leadership Club.
> We have so much.
> He has so little.
> We can make a difference here."

Dad sighs.
        "We're taking him
        because you committed us and
        Ms Nelson has no room.
        Your mother agreed
        without discussing it with me?"

        "In the car this morning.
        Thank you, Dad, thank you.
        What do we do now?"

We look at each other.

KEVIN

Brittany calls at 11:30
the parents in bed.
She launches in.

"Your church minister was interested in Thabo?
Is he cool about helping?"

"Yeah," I answer.
"The Rev is always talking about
standing up for principles
creating a compassionate world
that stuff."

"Will you take me to church
tomorrow morning?"

"So. You've found God?"

"Don't be an idiot.
I just want to ask your Reverend
if I can talk to the congregation
about Thabo.
We pick him up from detention tomorrow
and I think we could get donations.
He's going to need legal help
if he's going to be allowed to stay,
and that costs money."

She hesitates.

"I know you don't like talking in public,
but it would sound better
if you stood up there with me.
They know you."

This does seem like a good way
to do the right thing,
but it's not just that I get nervous.
Public speaking makes me throw up.

"I'll stand there
if you do the talking,"
I tell her. I can't say no to Brittany.

"You have to introduce me,
but it can be short,"
she says.

Never any doubt
in her mind
that I'd do it.

She talks about this boy, this stranger,
as if he's her best friend.

Almost
makes me jealous.

Thabo

The strangers
from the airport
take me
out of the cold cement place.
*   The doors click*
*   behind us.*

People in uniforms
give me my bag
with my extra shirts
my sister's photograph
a half pack of Benson and Hedges cigarettes
*   good for trading*
all I have
in this world.

I hold it tight
against my chest.

The quiet car
is like a dream
white faces turn towards me
tires swish
on smooth wet tarmac

then a house
little white fence
a garden
*   full with flowers*
*   that could grow*
*   a month of vegetables*

a little dog
with a curly tail
too friendly for guarding

hard, shining floor as we walk in
carpet on the stairs
so thick my feet sink into it

a room just for me
with a soft, clean bed
a closet full of more clothes
than I ever had before

their words slide around
until I understand them

> *"This will be yours,"*
> *they tell me,*
> *"until we sort this out."*

They give me all these things

I wonder
what they will want
in exchange.

KEVIN

Brittany calls me over
after Thabo arrives.

When I get there
everyone is sitting in the living room
on the edge of their chairs.
The dog leans against Leah's leg
whines.

I can taste tension.

Brittany sits beside Thabo.
He's tall and skinny
with a baby face and smooth dark skin.
Looks like a kid but his eyes are old.

He looks around,
past the shoulder of the person who talks to him,
over his own shoulder
behind him.

Probably just confused.
I get that.
Either he doesn't know much English
or he doesn't want to talk.
I get that too.
Brittany does enough talking for everyone.

He dips his head and says
over and over
"Eh, ntate, eh, aussi."

The whole family walks him
around the house,
shows him his room.
Brittany's mom opens the dresser
underwear,
socks, t-shirts, jeans,
a pair of runners.
In the closet
a sweatshirt and jacket.

He looks around, eyes wide.
They look back
expectantly.

Brittany

His eyes shine white
against his dark skin.

It's harder to talk to him
than I thought.
He doesn't understand English.
But he's polite.
He looks at me when I talk.

Taking him around the house
is like that home makeover TV show,
the one where they blindfold the owner,
then they take off the blindfold
and show her
how they turned her dump of a house
into this designer place
with a few thousand dollars
and smart decorating moves.

He bobs his head
smiles
       I thought he'd be more emotional
       more grateful
       but whatever.

I'm bringing him
to school next week
to get him started on his missed education
to show him to everyone.

I leave Leah and Kevin to keep him company
while I go online to organize
tomorrow's Global Leadership club meeting.

Ms Nishi, our sponsor teacher, will be excited.
The club executive will be impressed.
They'll all listen to me.
It'll be cool.

Leah

I speak
slowly and clearly
so Thabo can understand.

"You come from Africa.
Now you stay here."

He nods at me. "Yes, seestah."

Awkward silence.
Kevin and I look at each other,
back at Thabo.

"You like Canada?" I ask.
A shiver passes through his body
and he wraps his arms around himself,
blows out his cheeks,
snorts.

I understand perfectly.
He thinks it's cold.

We all laugh.

I show him the bathroom.
"You want a bath? Wash? Hot water?"
He smiles, nods, murmurs.

"Eh, ah-oosy. Yes seestah. Wash."

"Eh," I say, "That's Canadian.
I guess we speak some of the same language."

I bring him a fresh towel,
new clothes.
Kevin has started running the tub.
Thabo is pulling off his old shirt
as Kevin and I back out the door.

"This will be a big change,"
Kevin says
"Are you ready for it?"

I shrug. "Have to be, I guess.
It's happening."

Kevin looks at me, smiles.
He looks like my manga boy sketches.

I hold my breath
as my heart bumps.

He heads down the hall
towards Brit's room
and I breathe again.

Thabo stays in the water a long time.
When I pass the bathroom,
I hear his deep hum, splashing.
This won't be so hard, I think.

Later, when he's done,
dressed in his new clothes,
we gather at the kitchen table.
Supper is roast chicken, potatoes and salad.

Thabo eats steadily
grips his fork like a weapon.

Our family conversation
eddies around him.

Brittany

It is a little tense
having Thabo in the house.

He's hard to talk to

and last night
he called out
in his sleep
from his room.

I heard Mom or Dad
get up
a couple of times
listen
outside the door
until he was quiet again.

I had to put a pillow
over my ears.

I'm sorry he has nightmares
but
I need my sleep.

Leah

In detention
the immigration people
figured out Thabo's language –
Sotho,
spoken by some tribes
in southern Africa.

I type a few key words
into an online translator
practice the pronunciation
with the computer voice,
make notes,

look up Sotho-speaking countries
on Wikipedia.

His language
his life
is such a different landscape
such a different world

but we can communicate.

KEVIN

Brittany and Leah
walk on either side of Thabo
like bodyguards.

I meet them at the school gate
and we thread our way
through parent cars
as they inch forward
drop their kids at the front door.

We get looks.

Brittany tosses her hair
smiles at her public
grips Thabo's arm
guides him forward.

They walk ahead
like a couple.

Brittany

We walk Thabo
into the school
through a crowd
of students.

Of course
they've all heard the story
seen the posts.

I feel him shrink
as the crowd presses closer.
      I know how it feels
         to be the centre of attention.
         You get used to it
         even get to like it.

Voices bounce
off the high ceiling of the rotunda.
More eyes look down
from the mezzanine.

Thabo tugs at my hand, pulls back
towards the door
towards Leah,
behind us.

But I know how to deal with this
      embrace it
        don't run from it.
I grip his arm
pull him into the middle of the crowd.

"C'mon Thabo. We got this.
Let's make a scene."

Leah

Ahead, I see Brit pull Thabo
into the crowd.
I push forward,
touch his shoulder
whisper in his ear,
"Ho lokile, it's okay."

At my awkward words,
Thabo's head swings towards me
face splits in a warm smile.

Brittany knows her audience
but she doesn't know Thabo.

On my spare today
I need to learn
more vocabulary.

KEVIN

Brittany knows how
to work a crowd.
She gathers them around her
presses Thabo forward
so they can all see him.
He looks like
a scared puppy.

"So everybody,
this is the boy who was stranded
at the airport.
His name is Thabo,
that's 'Taa – bo.'
He doesn't know much English,
so he'll be in ELL class to start with.
Please be nice to him.
Don't forget to donate to the Thabo Defence fund
and come to the Global Leadership work sessions
later this week."

She dazzles a smile,
waves a hand at questions.
"Later," she says,
and they drift away.

Thabo looks around the sun-lit lounge
at the wrought-iron railing on the mezzanine above,
at students who sit on carpeted stairs,
at folding tables,
on cement ledges
eating giant breakfast cookies from the cafeteria,
focused on their phones or game consoles.

Pop music blares from the loudspeakers.
Thabo looks dazed.

For a second I see the school
through his eyes,
overwhelming.

Then I look back at Brittany
killer body,
perfect, shiny hair,
confident tilt of her head.

Hard to see
anything else.

Leah

Brit has Global Leadership class
so she hands Thabo over to me
to take upstairs to the English Language Learner class.

It's decorated with posters
of Canada and language skills
fewer kids
than my over-full regular classes.

Most students are Chinese,
two Arabic boys,
an Indian girl from my Phys Ed class,
a couple of white kids who look Russian,
a knot of Filippinos
a girl with very black skin in a hijab.

The students speak to each another
in broken English.
It sounds strange.
The hallways are alive
with multiple languages.
Everyone hangs out
in their own language groups,
unless they're forced
to cross the lines.

Mrs. Lo directs Thabo to a desk
and the class falls silent,
watching.

I hand Thabo his pencil case and binder,
touch his hand.
"Ho lokile."

A smile ghosts across his face.
"Eh, is good."

Thabo

My head buzzes
with the new things
I see this morning.

The students talk
when the teacher turns
to write on the white board.
She does not get angry.

It is different here.
No uniforms
no textbooks or worksheets,
no school fees,
no quiet classroom.

I don't understand
what the teacher wants.

I don't know
what will happen next.

I sit quietly.
Maybe
no one will notice
me.

Leah

In Science
it's hard to concentrate
on invasive species,
even though the Australian cane toad movie
is totally gross.

I worry
that Thabo is freaked out.
Will the others gang up on him?
He's so skinny.
Can he defend himself?

I pencil in the last
cloze notes,
tune out the teacher.

On my way to French,
I detour past Thabo's classroom.
He sits
staring at the desk.
I wave but
he doesn't see me.

Brittany

In Socials class
I rock.
We discuss refugees
citizenship
human rights.

Ms Nelson is turning Thabo
into a lesson
and everyone listens to me
make connections.
I can tell she's excited
by the energy in the class.

She hands out a blank chart
on immigration
headlined with an Inquiry Question
links to Big Ideas in italics
Curricular Competencies in bullet points.

Ms Nelson claps her hands
bounces on her toes.
"Now, everyone,
to the library!
Remember
Today we'll go through the stages
of Find, Filter and Focus
in our research process."

All that stuff is lame
but I'm okay with it.
It *is* my project.

Leah

Kevin is in French class before me.
He waves me over.

Usually I sit on my own at the front
advanced two years
because of summer French camps.

I can do the work
but the older kids banter
back and forth.
They scare me.

I smile at Kevin
show too many teeth
slide into the desk beside his,
sit straight
on the edge of my chair.

His skin is golden brown,
his thick black hair
flops over his forehead.

"How's the new brother?"

His dark eyes distract me,
and I cough before I reply.

"Quiet. Hungry. Confused."
I tell Kevin about his wordlessness
his language
our charades
and laughter,
my go-to phrase, *"Ho lokile."*

"Hey," he says, "like *The Lion King*.
Hakuna matata, no worries."

But that's not true for Thabo.
I explain about the nightmares
the haunted eyes.
"He seems…damaged."

Kevin listens, nods,
seems to understand.

"Dad says he has demons,
but he's okay with it.
Dad's home all day anyway
writing.
Mom just launches herself
into the cause,
like Brittany."

Kevin's face softens.
"Yeah. Like Brittany."

I can't believe
I've talked so much

cover my lips
with my fingers.

Brittany's crazy
not to see Kevin not only likes her
but *really* likes her.

It's wasted on Brittany.
She dabbles in boyfriends
never keeps them long.

I would appreciate
a reaction
like that
to my name

especially from Kevin.

Madame Robert clears her throat.
"Bonjour, tout le monde. Ca va bien?"
We both face front.

Now I have to concentrate

with Kevin beside me.

KEVIN

French homework
done fast
in my spare.
Leah's explanation
made the *l'imperatif* exercise easy.

I turn to my laptop.

An online report
on abandoned minors
leaves more questions.
Is Thabo legally a separated
or abandoned child?

Is the old woman
a "person of concern"?

How old is he
and can he prove it?

Where does he go from here?

Back to the place
that gave him nightmares?

Thabo

I went to school
in my village
for some few years.

In my home
school was serious.
The teachers frowned
yelled
punished me for laughing.

I wanted to go past Form 2
to make a better life
but school fees
and uniforms
cost more
than my mother made.

Then she died
and I had to learn
to care
for myself.

My older sister
went her own way.

In Canada
the teacher talks
in a friendly voice,
smiles kindly.

This building is beautiful.
Light shines through windows in the roof,

desks and chairs,
computers for everyone,
and someone else
who cleans up.

Students sigh
and roll their eyes
when we have work to do.

How do they learn
when it is all
so easy?

Brittany

We send Thabo home
with Leah
stay late at the Leadership meeting.

They love my Thabo memes and posters
especially now
they've seen him
for real.

"This is like the best campaign ever!"
Courtenay gushes.
I can always count on her.

We need cash for a lawyer,
more than bake sales
and carwashes
can give us.

I start a publicity committee
plan a GoFundMe page;
they all want to help.
Kevin will find the media contacts
We'll all blitz our networks
maybe start an online petition.
We'll get the city lit.

The money will start to flow.
I'm good at this.

KEVIN

We leave school in the rainy dark
walk fast to my car
close the doors
against the wind-whipped wet leaves
settle into the leather seats.

"Remember those designer clothing ads?"
Brittany says,
"Black and white people together?
We need some just like that
of Thabo and me."

I wonder where this is going.
"Okay."

"And you too
cause you're Chinese."

"Yes, I am."

She relaxes as the seat heater kicks in.
"We can get an angle on this
a media campaign
of the modern
inclusive
multicultural
socially responsible
high school.
And we're all good looking."
"Thanks," I say,
but I know
it's not a compliment.
It's a strategy.

The engine purrs
as we ease out of the parking lot.
I shake off the weird,
bounce questions off Brittany.
"I need to know
how Thabo got into Canada.
Did the old woman claim refugee status?
Who is she?
Where is she?
Is she part
of some child trafficking scheme?"
Brit turns to me, her eyes wide.
"Wouldn't that be great?"

I look at her.

"No, really.
I mean, like,
social media
would be all over that."

Brittany talks
the rest of the way to her house.

I drive.

She doesn't notice
I don't answer.

Leah

He gets what I say
mostly.
When he talks
he swears.
Obscenities
pepper his sentences.

When we puzzle them out
my mother's head pulls back
eyebrows pinch.

Brittany laughs out loud.

"Now Rebecca, it's what he knows,"
my dad soothes.
She holds her hand
to her forehead.

Thabo's eyes flit
from one to another
then to me
worry on his forehead.

"*Ho lokile,*" I assure him.
"You'll get more words soon,
better words.
These ones are ugly."

His face smooths.
He nods
as if he understands.

Brittany

Thabo makes a good
poster boy.

Facebook icons, retweets
Instagram shares
spread his picture
and my slogans
through the networks.

Even the newspaper
puts a photo of me
and Thabo
on the front of the local news section.
The article is long
gives a bunch of legal stuff,
boring

but our picture
looks awesome.

We have collection boxes at school and Kevin's church
to pay for the paperwork
or the lawyer
or something.

Homerooms are competing
for who can raise the most cash.
Winners get a class pizza party.

I've set them all
on fire.

Leah

In computer drafting class
I watch Kevin at the computer
fingers flying
eyes focused on the screen.

His hands curl over the keyboard
like question marks.
He flicks his hair
out of his eyes.

Magic flows from
his flashing fingers.

Huh
he grunts in triumph
as his 3D object spins
on the screen.

KEVIN

My parents
demand progress reports.
Calculus quiz
English essay
Chemistry lab
Computer Science project.
Results.

Only 92? Study harder.
We didn't move here
sacrifice our lives
leave your grandparents
for you to waste time
on clubs
posters
refugees.
You have bigger goals.

They've set their own goals,
told me they're mine.

This country is too soft.
Refugees
who believes the stories?
We work hard
make sacrifices.
Why can't they?

I tell them about Thabo
left at the airport
hungry
illiterate
washed up on the shores
of the baggage carousel.

They sniff.
Let in one
they grow like bamboo
spread through the country
don't work, collect money.

Helping them
makes us weak.

I turn to my computer.
I know they want me to succeed
to make their sacrifices worthwhile

but we have different ideas
about what that means.

I'm not gonna change their minds.
I pick my battles
and this isn't one of them.

Brittany

When Leah talks to him
Thabo's eyes light up.
She's learned words
in his language.
When she leaves the room
he watches for her return.
I'm just another
pretty face.

My sister
always was a smart
ass.

I call Kevin over.
He comes running.

The Reverend

In the front pew
a row of youth group members
alive with mission
Kevin's beautiful young friend
and the refugee boy
in their ranks.

Beside Kevin, a woman my age
short blonde hair, strong jaw
tailored red jacket over black slacks
professional even on Sundays,
watches through dark eyes.

In the middle
grey-haired ladies
nod approvingly as the words
pour like a baptismal flood
gurgling of despair
exploitation
victims

and doing the right thing.

Husbands
wait out the sermon
until the reward,
tea and cookies.

Ms Nelson

He looks more like
an outdoor guide
than a minister of the Lord,
long arms
red hair turning white
blue eyes in a tanned face.
A scent of cedar
clings to his robe.
Is he wearing hiking boots?

He grips the pulpit
leans forward for momentum.

Sermon over, his call to action settling
over the congregation,
he announces the hymn.

Brittany rises beside me at Kevin's nudge
The congregation sings
with the choir
     Let the flame of love burn higher
     This is a church on fire.

During community announcements
Brittany, Kevin and Thabo walk to the front.
Kevin stares at the floor, mumbles an introduction.

Surely I've taught him better speaking skills than that.

Brittany bubbles with energy
holds Thabo's arm possessively,
explains his situation
flashes smiles, tosses her hair,
rolls her eyes disarmingly.

The whole congregation
longs to open their hearts
and their wallets.
Thabo nods
smiles shyly.
"Thank you," he says.
We are charmed.

Leah

Mom raises her eyebrows
as I lean over my plate.
"Leah, are you working too hard, honey?"

I straighten,
hiding my fatigue after a Sunday afternoon
of Kinect baseball
at Alisha's empty house
instead of finishing Math homework.

I turn back to black bean chili
and her concern.
"I'm okay, Mom. Just some Math to do."
Under the table
Yoko leans against my leg,
hoping for scraps.

I ask Mom about her shift last night.
She launches into stories
of a myocardial infarction,
a fatal three-car collision,
a lonely senior
with indigestion.
Brittany and Dad add commentary
then Brittany talks about church
and the flow of donations
after their appearance.

Across the table
Thabo grips his spoon
scoops up chili,
eats hunks of French bread in two bites.

After three weeks
he still doesn't do
dinner conversation.

Late at night, Math done,
I pass the open door of his room
on my way to bed.
It's dark and quiet.

Later, as I drift off
I hear from his room
a wire-thin wailing.

Brittany

The coins and bills
flow in
first in a trickle
then
as Thabo's sweet shy smile wins hearts,
in a flood.

The appeal spreads
as I knew it would
through glossy posters
Facebook photos
Twitter feeds
a couple of YouTube videos
taken with a cell phone
in the school rotunda.

But we can do better.

Leah

Brittany's wired
when she gets home from school,
her cheeks flushed
with success.

Looks like we've got enough
for a lawyer
or maybe someone will do it
pro bono.

As if she knew
what that was
before Kevin told her.

Thabo kicks off his shoes
as soon as he walks in
settles on his haunches
holds out a hand
to the dog's eager adoring face.

Thabo

A man
in a blue suit
asks me questions.
Ms Nelson says he is a lawyer.

I tell him

the old woman told me to say
she was my grandmother
took my passport
my identification papers
said she would return
very soon
left me at the baggage place.

I tell him

I don't know
my date of birth.
I lived on the street
slept in doorways
got food
where I could find it
stole
when it was necessary.

I am careful
not to tell him

the bad things.

Ms Nelson

Immigration writes
to me as Designated Representative
tells me their
x-rays
measurements
tests
while inconclusive
suggest Thabo could be
over 18
a legal adult
not subject to protection
as an abandoned child.
They've taken into account
the effects of malnutrition
lack of medical care
in determining age.

It creates the illusion
of youth, they say.

As an adult
he is subject
to deportation legislation.
No papers
no identity
no legal entry.

"Please report to the nearest Immigration Centre
on the last day of this month
for removal."

Removal

like garbage
or a tumour
just get rid of it,
clean up.

The signature at the bottom
is a hasty scrawl.

KEVIN

Brittany refuses
to accept the Immigration ruling
decides we need an internet video campaign.

TV news cameras
visit the school
interview the principal
follow Thabo from class to class.
Brittany brings me with her
to the interview.
The reporter's complexion
is unnaturally smooth,
her eyes outlined in dark pencil,
lips perfectly red.
Her gaze is everywhere but us
until the red camera light comes on.

I stand beside Brit
nod over and over
as she explains
the airport abandonment
immigration rules
Thabo's acceptance in school
the horror that might await him
in his home country.

Brittany sounds totally confident.
"Our goal is to cover legal costs,
give our new friend some hope."
The reporter turns to me.
I'm a deer in the headlights.
"And you, young man?
I understand you're the research whiz."

My heart stops.
Brittany tugs my sleeve
and my heart starts again with a stutter
as I look down at her.
"I'm just the technology."
Pause.
"He's um a good kid.
I hope I can uh help him.
How uh whatever."

The camera swings away to the reporter
who takes over with no hesitation
in a voice much bigger
than she is.

Leah

Cell phone video works
but I borrow
the good camera
from the photo teacher
learn the buttons
wires
zoom
boom mike
principles of good filming.
Brittany is coordinating
something else
so I'm the director
camera operator
screenwriter
interviewer.

Already the profile is high
so I'd better make it
good.

At night I draw a storyboard
sketch madly
as images flow
from my pencil
blur into a story
on the page.

Ms Nelson

Weeks
after our return
the luminous dial
of the clock radio
wakes me
at 3 a.m.

Until fingers of light reach across the sky
my thoughts chase each other
like mice in a wheel
the boy's liquid eyes
airport officials' starched shirts
my history curriculum
that never changes,
my comfortable
predictable life.

The end of the month is approaching.
I have to make a decision.

I reach for my phone.

The Reverend

The teacher
Miranda Nelson
phones me early.
My eyes struggle open.

Her voice is full
of intensity.
"I have a proposal
for you and your church.
Do you remember Thabo?"

        "Of course."

 "We've received a letter.
We have until the end of the month.
And then he'll be deported."

I stutter with indignation
anger rising
like a wave.

She outlines her plan.

I know it's been done before.
We can keep him in the church,
offer sanctuary.
Police will respect the tradition.
At the least
we'll get a delay.

I fumble for my glasses
scribble her number
details.

My heart races, hand shakes.

Her voice
steadies me.

KEVIN

Ms Nelson keeps me
after school
tells me I have a new research project.

"But I'm busy with...

She interrupts.
"And this is
all about that."

She wants information on
church sanctuary cases,
precedent, tradition, practice,
case law.
It all counts.

"I'd like you
to put a list together."

"I can try."

She tilts her head
to look through the bottom
of her glasses,
raises her eyebrows.

"There's a mark in it
for you."

The Reverend

I still pause
in wonder
at God's infinite variety
as I look out at my multi-coloured flock.

In my northern home town
there were the white kids
the kids of relocated Japanese families
who seemed as white as we were
a few Indo-Canadian kids whose dads worked at the mill
And the Native kids (we call them First Nations now)
who mostly
kept to themselves.
We regarded each other
with suspicion.

I never met a black or Jewish person
until I went on exchange
to Quebec as a teen
with a group from Toronto.

Little did I imagine
        riding the trails
        on horseback in summer
        snowmobile in winter

that I would no longer be
of the unnoticing majority
that our world would require
negotiation
re-evaluation
the dance of accommodation
for differences.

It seemed simple
from cowboy country
that all you needed to get along
was a grin and a shrug
a strong moral compass
and Church on Sundays
to meet girls

chalk one up towards
the Greater Good.

Brittany

Almost a full-time job
keeping track of
    interviews
    fundraisers at school
    Kevin's church
    Parent Advisory Council meetings.
Ms Nelson helps me
set up a donation account
at the Royal Bank
and every time I check
the money has doubled.

I write captions
update every couple of hours
take photos
everywhere

The one with
Kevin, Thabo and me
looks like an ad for GAP
or a kids' show
or a government ad
for the Multicultural Act.

My dad is going to help
writing press releases.
There's hardly time to go to school.

I steal half an hour
to play piano in the family room.
The music washes over me
and the world disappears.

When I look up
Thabo stands in the doorway to the kitchen
watching wordlessly.

Thabo

At my home
we make music
with our voices
our drums
the mbira
the guitar.

Music and dancing
make me at peace
with the world
for a little while.

This music
from Brittany's fingers
speaks a new language.

I understand it.

Leah

The river thick with silt
shredded with wind waves
makes a good backdrop.
We set up the tripod
I adjust controls.
Thabo's face comes into focus
gazing at the water.

"Now," I tell him, "start talking."
His smile flashes white
across his brown face.

"Eh, aussi.
I come from Africa.
My grandmother, she is gone.
I have no family
My life back home is very dangerous.
I ask to stay in Canada."

I film him walking the boardwalk
approaching from the front
walking away
lots of time for voice-over.

We pass historical information signs
tasteful black and white photos
of grinning fish cannery workers
bunkhouses assigned by race
all immigrants
except the First Nations bunkhouse.

Thabo's jeans are still new
his legs long and lean.

He huddles in his jacket
collar turned up
against the cold.

Looks good on camera.

Behind him the river
rushes by.

I click the record button off.
"Ho lokile," I say.
"That's good for now."

Thabo

The teacher Ms Nelson
and the lawyer
come to the house in the afternoon
after school

tell me

the government gave her a letter.
They want to send me back.

I am afraid.
In my home country
the police will be waiting
with their cages
their black clubs
their guns.

The lawyer tells me they will fight
the order.
But how do you fight a government?
How can you change their mind?

I am afraid to trust them
with the whole truth

that I have done
very bad things

that I don't deserve
saving.

Leah

I sit with Thabo
after dinner
in the living room.

He is trying to absorb news
of the deportation order.
I can see him pulling back
into a shell
all the tendrils he sent out
to put down roots
scorched.

"Is there anyone?" I ask.
"Where is your mother? Your father?"

"'*M'e oa ka*, my mother, she passed away
of wasting disease.
Ntate oa ka, my father,
he passed away
by gunshot.

"I live on the streets
with my gang,
then *'m'e moholo*
comes to me
says she will give me a good life
when we arrive in Canada."

I can think of so many reasons
she wanted him
none of them for
a good life
in Canada.

KEVIN

My research on sanctuary
turns up some cool history.
"Last resort of the desperate,"
the internet story says.

The government site declares,
they will enforce deportations.
"No one is exempt from the law,"

but Border Services say
it looks bad
to break into a church
slap handcuffs on refugees
drag them into the glare of day.

News channel archives
give background on sanctuary
as a centuries-old tradition of church vs state
parallel authorities.

Seems we still respect
or fear
God

but the government sets limits,
whatever the optics,
and grants no appeals, states in a policy document:
"Disproportionate publicity for church sanctuary
means there are questions about the clearing process.
Murderers and terrorists
don't deserve sanctuary
and churches can be naive."

The government promises
to fast-track refugee claims,
cut down talk and time.
"We'll get it right
the first time,
no delays, no appeal"

and no second chances.
Refugees hide
in church basements.
Outside on the sidewalk

the police wait.

Leah

My dad says
that I have too much screen time
takes me across the road
to the ball diamond,
lobs pitches
that I smack to the fence
before I run the bases.

My feet pound
body leans around second base
as the dog fetches the ball
runs it back.

I race around third
slide into home
under my dad's glove.

I get up
brush sand off my sweats
panting.
I grin at him in triumph.

He grins back.
All part of our game.

Ms Nelson

The tide of students
swirls in and out
of my classroom.

Paper piles up
in my "to be filed" tray
Online school discussion forum
nags about unread messages.

My desk, normally pristine
        daybook open
        paperclips and pens in appropriate sections
        of the stationery organizer,
now shows the ragged edge of chaos
        unmarked papers
        untouched staff surveys
        undistributed notices for homeroom.

When I lift the lid on my laptop
school work fades
as I lose myself
in planning rescue.

I've spent my life
teaching the value of the rule of law
of peace, order and good government.

The Canadian Council of Churches reminds me,
"It's our moral obligation
to oppose unjust laws."

The government wants to filter out the dangerous
but Thabo has no legal identity.
He doesn't exist
ergo he has to go.

The Reverend has a spark
of defiance
that is re-igniting in me.
If we obey authorities
there's no question
injustice will be done.

Leah

Internet tutorials
teach me details
of iMovie editing.

In French class
we finish work fast
and Kevin explains
special effects.

At home
in the family room
Brittany practices piano
runs the hard parts
of her exam pieces
over and over.

In Mom's office
it's background music.

Kevin and I huddle over the iMac
late into the night
bringing Thabo alive
on screen

while he sleeps.

KEVIN

Our YouTube video
seeps through the social networks
linked, liked, shared,
tweeted, copied, imitated,
animated into
a rude spoof
that's pulled down
but not before catching on,
spreading like fire.

Every day the views count leaps.
The city, the country, the world
can't get enough of him.

"It's official," Brittany tells me
"It's gone viral."

Ha! Did it! I text Leah.

Ya she replies
**Everyone's talking. T's famous.
Will it make a difference?**

DK I text back
Have to wait and see.

The Reverend

Worship is growing,
wooden pews crowded with young people
coat rack outside
jammed with hoodies and goretex.

I invite the little children
to the front early
to make more space for the grey-haired couples.
The new arrivals lift my spirits.

Kevin's teacher, Miranda, is back
sitting straight
shoulders back
in her red jacket
her eyes alert.

The sermon this morning
is "Jesus, the Rebel".
Miranda listens carefully,
nods at important points.
The elders are politely attentive
the teens listen, squirm, swing their feet.
a few smile as I speak.

Everyone sings to the gospel hymn
"It only takes a spark."

I gauge my success by raised eyebrows
raised voices.

Shows they're listening
even if they don't agree.

Ms Nelson

I attend church
twice in a month.
Haven't done that since childhood.

After the service
I head to the vestry
with the minister.
He swings off his robe
hangs it in the closet.
I was right.
He wears black hikers.

He shows me the space
cot, toilet, shower
small windows
glazed with privacy glass.

Thabo will be cramped
confused
afraid
but better this
than a one-way ticket
into the clutches
of abusers.

The kids can visit
help him with schoolwork
and English
provide him with company
and comfort.

He'll be safe here.

Brittany

I click off the elliptical trainer,
step down onto the cushioned gym floor
calculate a five-minute shower
before I head across the park to the high school.

The warm water
sluices off the sweat
and sleep
that ended too soon.

Up late with an essay on John Milton for English
constant velocity lab in Physics
studying for a Geography quiz on human migration.

The possibility
that Thabo could be kicked out
pisses me off.
All that work!

Kevin is researching options.

The lawyer has lots to say
but not many suggestions
for what to do.

Ms Nelson has something up her sleeve
And I have a radio interview
after school today.
Leah's doing clips of the video
for YouTube shorts.

We all do what we're good at.

KEVIN

Leah is nothing
like her sister
no flounce
or pout
or clever smiles over her shoulder,
no excited chatter.

Her voice is quiet
focused on the task
French verbs
iMovie editing techniques
YouTube hits.

Her eyes
rarely meet mine,
flicker away.

On the outside she's calm water
but I feel the pull
of undercurrents.

The Reverend

The church board members
listen carefully
to my presentation on social gospel.
I quote church circulars on refuge.
They nod, frown,
look uncomfortably at each other
when I ask that we take on the boy's case,
offer sanctuary.

In this tidy
well-kept suburb
they are used to deciding
the night for the community dinner
Palm Sunday decoration budgets
fundraising options,
the successful candidate
for junior minister.

This request for refuge
defying a government order
makes them squirm
in their cushioned chairs.

Thabo

In my home dogs are slinking
fierce creatures

They steal your food
snarl, snap, bite.
People keep them
for protection
hit them until they're vicious
call them "Simba."

I throw rocks
when they roar at me
like death.

Here, the dog is a little wriggling animal
that wags its whole body
tongue lolling out
eyes crinkling.
It sits on my feet.

I lean down, touch its head
its curly tail
thick reddish fur soft under my hand.
It loves me.

Small, weak.
How does it survive?

Ms Nelson

It all comes down to definitions
The boy is a pawn of circumstance
and certainly needs emergency assistance.

Refugee claims have a process
a step-by-step system,
each requiring documentation.

We have learned so little about him.
Leah tells us
Thabo's life has been one of survival
his parents lost when he was a child
on the street as a youngster
the only support his street gang.
Who knows
what he went through?

Hard to know
if he will ever be legal here.
In this bureaucratic jungle
paper is the king.

I have always admired
the measured
documented way of our world

but sometimes
clearly
we need exceptions.

Thabo

I keep my secrets
no names
no details
that might identify me
or them.

If they know
about the fire
they will never let me stay
(the old woman told me
never to speak of it).

At night
I dream of running
dogs snarling at my heels
hands on my body
rough, demanding, punishing.
I waken in the soft bed
to my own crying.

Leah

The cold air hits my face
like a slap,
the morning dog walk
along the river an endurance test.

When Yoko stops to sniff
I pull out my phone
fingers too cold
to work the touch screen.

Driving rain
stirs a chop in the murky river.

I tug the leash
hurry along.

The border police will be coming tomorrow
and we've got to get Thabo
to sanctuary.

Not much light
in this dark day.

KEVIN

My friends text me, tell me
I'm getting boring
no time to hang out
shoot baskets in open gym afternoons
go to games
get to the next level in Warcraft.

When the classroom door closes
I head to the school lounge
pull out my smart phone
reply to legal aid message boards
research the school library legal databases.

Tangled language, precedents,
current cases, prerequisites,
exceptions, compassionate grounds.
There must be a way
through this jungle.

When my mom asks
if I'm doing homework
I say
I'm studying law.
She nods and smiles.

I visit Leah and Thabo
try to get more details
something to pry open
the legal box he's in.

Ms Nelson

The drizzle pounds the windshield
as I turn off the wipers,
washes smoothly down
the polished fenders of my Fiat.

I sit for a minute
breathe in the smell
of leather seats
secure in my bubble,

windows tightly sealed
against the rain.

I'm thrown by the early morning,
before I left
a knock at the apartment door
a Priority Post courier
with a letter from Border Services.

With no status in Canada,
Thabo will be escorted to the airport
tomorrow
for deportation.
Home is wherever they decide it to be.

I breathe deeply
straighten my shoulders
crack the door handle.

The rain trickles in.

Brittany

I flop on my bed
turn my head to look down on the park
from my top floor bedroom window.
The door closed on my English project group,
I click "Save As,"
upload the presentation to the Cloud.
Hope the teacher's ancient laptop
will run the program version we need.
Presentation is due tomorrow
and we just squeaked
under the deadline.

Impatience bubbles through me
Paradise Lost
History quiz
What do they matter
when maybe tomorrow
it all falls apart?

Everyone expects me to save the world.
I'm trying as hard as I can.
What if it's not enough?

I need to chill
sit down at my piano.

I play "Für Elise"
till confidence
fills me again.

Part 3

Leah

I try to explain about the law
the Border Services Agency
how church sanctuary works

but I don't think
Thabo gets it.

He only gets
that he has to go.

He packs his new clothes
into his new backpack.

We walk the river boardwalk
one last time.
Yoko trots beside him.
The wind picks up,
tossing waves
like white horses galloping.
The empty branches
of the ornamental cherry trees
rattle in the wind.

Thabo tucks into his jacket,
pulls down his toque.

"You're getting used to the cold,"
I tell him.
I'm trying to be positive.
"You're learning to be Canadian."

His eyes slant towards me,
"No," he says
"They don't allow me stay."

I fling my arm
around his shoulders
thin even in a puffy jacket
hug him close.
He hugs me back.

"It's not over yet,"
I tell him.

KEVIN

We go together
in Brit's parents' van
Ms Nelson, Leah, Brittany, Thabo, me, Brit's dad

park in the underground garage
make our way upstairs
just as evening worship
lets out.

The secretary leads Thabo
into the back room.
He looks around.

"Maybe I can be safe,"
he says to me,

turns to Leah.
"Maybe after
I can be Canadian."

She slides her arm around him,
smiles crookedly.
"We're trying."

The Reverend

The Thabo contingent arrives early
The congregation is electrified by the news.
They stream out, seeking a glimpse
of this here and now
outreach ministry
the word made flesh
faith come to life.

The pews have filled
parishioners crowding together,
sharing hymn books
filling the offering envelopes.

The boy is quiet, slim,
big-eyed and sharp-boned
a poster-child pin-up of needy
right in front of them.

Who could resist?

We're united
in a mission
to be saviours.

Ms Nelson

The wary look had begun to fade
but now it's back
in his eyes

like a cat when it slips outside
the shiver of wildness
descending
awakening nerve endings
senses alert to danger.

He seems to understand
he has to stay here
that the church
keeps the law at bay
a last attempt
at refuge.

The Reverend

Thabo has become my shadow.
He rises early
runs on the treadmill
donated by a member of the congregation.
When I arrive he's showered
eagerly awaiting
the daily tasks.

He cares for flowers
sweeps the hall
sets up chairs
studies the *Stories of Jesus*
comic books
in the Sunday School room.

After school
Kevin and Leah arrive.
They design lessons
borrow exercises from their teachers
plan to fill in the gaps
of his survivalist childhood
English basics
world geography
numbers.

Leah's iPad hums
YouTube education videos
map games
past imperfect
and future tense.

KEVIN

We're trying to pin down
where he comes from
show pictures of different countries
cities
landscapes.

The best we can do is Southern Africa
Maybe Lesotho
Botswana,
South Africa
but he shrugs off names.

For someone who seems
so helpless,
so innocent,
he is weirdly evasive.

Leah

Softball season
is inside,
until the light returns,
pitching clinic on Friday nights,
gym practice on Wednesdays.

I crouch in my catcher's gear
hidden by chest protector
caged helmet
hard plastic over my legs and feet.

The repetitive thunk
in the glove
soothes the leaping uncertainty
in my mind.

Curve ball, drop ball, fastball, knuckle ball,
whatever Nikki can chuck at me
is swallowed
in my long brown glove
and that satisfying smack.

My mind doesn't think.
Between my eye and my hand

an electric connection.

Ms Nelson

Despite my powerful sense
of cosmic justice
It's not easy to defy orders.

The adrenaline races through me
when the two broad-shouldered,
upright, uniformed officers
appear at my door.

"As Designated Representative
you are responsible for the actions of the applicant.
You have been ordered to comply."
The tallest one speaks
in a weighty monotone.

I believe in the law
teach its logic
the vital importance
of order.

I make my face determined
my refusal calm and collected,
in compliance with sanctuary guidelines.
The door clicks behind them.
Through the curtain I watch
the men
head to their police car.

I sink to a kitchen stool
heart racing
hands shaking.

Brittany

Katie can hardly reach
the piano keyboard
can't tell a C from an F
but her blonde curls
feet that swing from the piano bench
baby-toothed smile
always win her thunderous applause
at Christmas recitals.

Her dad hovers
video camera in hand
her mother beams
when Katie folds in a deep baby bow
pleased
with her halting performance,
with audience approval.

She doesn't practice,
doesn't like the piano.

I can't give her what piano gives me
a river of feeling
a world of forgetting.

I'm probably failing her
as a teacher
but her parents are happy
to pay my bill.

Leah

The December coffee house
dedicates all profits
to the Thabo Defence Fund.

Brittany gets Kyle,
a graduate from last year,

now a local music celebrity,
to do a set
so it brings in a big crowd.

Brittany plays
"The Lion Sleeps Tonight"
a switch from her usual style
the audience
is hushed to the end
then
bursts into applause.

She stands, bows
drinks it in.

I'm sorry
Thabo's not here
for it.

My parents clap
harder than anyone.
They're so proud.

Kevin sits with his friends
claps for Brittany
then looks over
catches my eye
grins.

The Reverend

Christmas season
is my rush hour.

Concerts
community outreach
late night service
       trying to make my sermon
       fresh but still traditional
       with a dash of exotic international
       enough
to bring the congregation
peace
love
understanding.

For the Christmas Eve service
the pews are bursting
the children act out
a modernized nativity scene
       with street kids
       teen parents
       a homeless shelter
       and a plastic baby
       that slips out of its white towel
       falls face first
       into the baby basket.

The adults laugh indulgently
sing "Silent Night"
bundle up against the cool air
as they walk through the skiff of snow
on the way to their heated cars.

I watch them go.

Behind me
Thabo calls
"Good night, Reverend Bob.
Happy Christmas,"
heads to his little room.

We're spending Christmas together
here. Tomorrow
some of the congregation
will drop in
with gifts and food.

Just like family.

"Good night, son,"
I say.

Thabo

After Christmas
and the loud explosions
of the New Year
the sun hides
behind grey clouds.

At my home,
this month after Christmas
is the one with sky so blue
it hurts your eyes,
when the sun covers my back
like a hot blanket

when the heat rises up
from the tarmac
in waves you can see.
Our bare feet burn.

In this country
January days are short and dark
the sun hides
day
after day
after day.

Every day
every day
the rain falls
bounces off the smooth pavement.

Only one window

is clear of coloured glass pictures.
I sit near it
look out at the rain
and the gray sky.

Sometimes I feel
like I am losing
myself

down the drain.

KEVIN

Chinese New Year
Pro-D Day at school
conveniently placed
to deal with the majority
of sleep-deprived Asian kids.

My parents make sure
the house is clean
the food is cooked
red envelopes
ready for distribution.

They insist I join them
in the extended family celebration
that lasts all night
eating, dancing, being polite to elders.
In the morning I stagger to my bed
pockets stuffed with lucky money.

This new year looms
portentous and menacing
a coiled snake
a crouching tiger
a hidden dragon.

The local paper puts out an advertising supplement
all the businesses wishing us all
Gung hay fat choy, Happy New Year.
For a few days
we're all Chinese.

My mother phones her family
in Hong Kong
where it's tomorrow.

Thabo

The church is soft, quiet, rich.
The carpet is red.
The room where I stay
better than anything I dreamed of
in the dark days.

I follow the Rev
help him sometimes.
Leah comes, sometimes with Kevin.
They teach me reading.

Sometimes I sit
on my bed
holding my head
when remembering comes.
It makes me want to hit
something hard
to make myself
hurt.

This morning
I pull open the front doors
to breathe new air.
Across the road two men
in uniforms
in a parked car
sit up when they see me,
reach for the door handles.
I let the doors whisper shut.

Brittany

As my fingers dance
over the piano keys
the music lets my thoughts wander.

It was easier to generate buzz
when things were happening.

Now that Thabo has settled
into the church
the news stories are snippets
in the "update" section.
The Facebook page still gets hits
likes, comments on the wall,

but we've lost momentum.

My piano piece ends
with two bars of satisfying
crashing
chords.

We need
an encore.

Ms Nelson

The winter rains are slackening.
Sunshine like shock treatment
slashes across the jewel-green grass
on the boulevard.

Sunday morning
I sip coffee
at the desk in my study,
organize end-term essays, still awaiting judgement
update the online report system
decipher the pencil-scratched numbers
coded with circles
highlighters
asterisks
transfer them to the implacable
neatness of the computerized mark program.

I haven't had this deadline crunch
since my first years of teaching.
My Sundays are usually reserved for yoga
coffee with friends
a brisk circuit of the running trail through the park across the road
an episode or two.

I unwind watching
neatly edited Newsworld documentaries,
distant injustices, tragedies, genocides
natural disasters, extinctions.
I sip good red wine
never more than one
eat California strawberries.

Lately my Sunday routine has become
more disturbing than soothing.
The voices from the speakers
the desperate faces on the flat screen
bracketed by commentary
from wind-tossed, khaki-clad journalists
creep into my living room
whisper in my ear
echo for hours.

KEVIN

The youth group
hits the cosmic bowling alley
late on a Saturday night.
Most of the regular members bring a friend.
"It's fun, not faith"
and we take over four lanes.

Brittany is at drama rehearsal
so I invite Leah.
We pair up with Mike and Josh.
At first she's a weak link
but within three frames
her delivery straightens out
her knees stop tangling.

She throws a strike with a crash
sends the pins flying
turns to me
throws her hands in the air
her face lit with joy
and for a second

she's beautiful.

The Reverend

Youth Group is growing
their energy focused
creating a magnetic force.

Thabo comes to meetings.
In the early days he sat quiet in the corner
his eyebrows rising when spoken to.
"Yes, yes," he replied to every question.

Now, weeks later, he has relaxed,
his eagerness for company
for the opening door
emerging like a butterfly.
Smiles split his face as they arrive.

I shrug into my tweed jacket
a concession to my position.

The discussion topic:
Be the change we want to see.

The kids lean into the circle
glance over at Thabo, interrupt
raise voices in excitement.

When we're done
we're wrung out
inspired
energized with good intent
and the power to make it happen.

The movie night social
is an afterthought.

Thabo is the best thing
that ever happened to this congregation.

Ms Nelson

I came to history through stories,
knights and castles as a toddler
pioneer explorer books and TV as a child
romantic bodice rippers as a teenager
then Russian epics, Egyptian sagas
Cold War spy thrillers.

Human lives driven by forces
beyond their control
but clear to see
from a distant future
where they were going.

I loved the dramatic irony,
knowing what would happen
when the people from history did not.

The world of my contemporaries
was still unformed,
unpredictable.

Dark forces swelled up unexpectedly
like a balloon
about to burst.

I avoided the uncertainty
of current events.
History stayed still.
I was in control.

It's unsettling
to step into action
when I don't know
where it will lead

but we've done it
now.

KEVIN

Leah sees them first
two uniformed cops
casual, sauntering
walking a beat
it seems.

But never before
on this suburban street.

Around here, cops drive
talk to schools about Internet safety
ride floats in the Salmon Festival Parade.

And when they turn
at the end of the block
saunter back
we know
it's a stake-out.

Leah

The church door opens.

The red carpet in the lobby
the hush and high ceilings
make me think of
Medieval cathedrals
built to intimidate
built to strike awe
into the hearts of the people.

Makes me want to resist.

Kevin's comfortable here
hardly pauses
fills the entry hall
with talk and laughter.
He calls it our night school job.

We juggle text books
reading materials
iPad and laptop.
Thabo is happy to see us.
His eyes crease as
a smile flashes.

"Hi, hi," he says.
I greet him back,
"*O pela joang.*" How are you?
"*Ke pela hantle,*" he replies, I'm well.

He leads us to the office
we use as a tutoring room.
His leg jitters
as he grips the pen
leans over the paper
scratches out words.

Thabo

This place is
too soft, too quiet.
I am becoming
a dull knife.

I learn reading and writing,
work through books
that make sense
with pictures.

Kevin tells me,
"Write every day."

Leah brings me a small, beautiful book
full of empty lined pages.
She wants me to fill it
with words
to tell her the truth
she would not understand.

At home I would have sold it.

Leah

I buy a decorated notebook
tell Thabo he should write
a little
in it every day
to me
or to himself.

It will help his English
I tell him.

I don't tell him
I want to hear
truths he can't express
any other way

truths we can use
to prove he belongs
here.

Brittany

Kevin spends time
on his computer,
with Thabo
and Leah.

I notice
he's not beside me.

It's annoying
when I need him
and he's somewhere else.

Leah

Dad and Mom
have a hard time
saying no to the government.
Something about
a lifetime of obedience
reputation
community.

I tell Brit
about their voices,
through the study door
torn, full of worry.

She waves it away.

"What are they worried about?
We know what we're doing."

Brittany

With Thabo in church sanctuary,
I throw myself into the campaign.

We hold a benefit concert
(I play piano)

We put on a skit
(Courtenay and I write it
I play the lead).

Makes for good buzz
and online pictures.

The school
the city
come alive with our goal
to save him.

Thabo's face plasters the walls of the school
the power poles on downtown streets
posts on every social media platform.
Our video is shared
over and over.

Leadership class talks of little else.

We are becoming legal experts
media darlings
fundraising fanatics.

We sell pizza
sushi
bubble tea
chocolate chip cookies

We sell
hope.

Thabo

I sit near the clear window

watch the road
and the bouncing rain.

From behind a truck
comes a silver car
that looks like so many here
except this one slows down
window open even in the cool air.

A camera looks at the church window
at me in it.

The camera drops,
pulls back.

In the shadows behind it
I think I see
the old woman.

My heart jumps
into my throat.
I step back
out of sight.

She has found me.

The Reverend

I've got used to the boy
hanging around.
It's been nearly four months
and he seems to have adjusted to church routine.

The church hall freezer is full of casseroles
      fried chicken
      dumplings
      sausages
      soup
      pasta
from the congregation's home cooks.

I see their pleasure
in making a difference.

At times I worry
about his murky past,
what he hasn't said
or wouldn't.

At times I wonder
when
how
it will all end.

A lot is riding on this young man
not just for him
but for us all.

Leah

His name
"Thabo"
means happiness.

At first, I thought it was
a perfect example
of irony.

Happiness in his life?
As a street kid
a victim of abandonment
if not trafficking?

But he tells me,
no,
all names have meaning in his country
but they are just names.

And his smile
his frequent, booming laugh
makes it true.

Ms Nelson

A voice from the past
breaks into my present

a call from my ex-husband
his mother in an accident
in hospital with a broken collarbone
but she'll be out soon.

I'll visit her this afternoon.

The Reverend

He seems quiet
unassuming
undemanding
harmless
but when he is alone
he is possessed
by rages
that come and go.

I hear from custodians
of crashing noises
but when they investigate
they find him
curled in his blankets.

Ms Nelson

My ex-mother-in-law
sits propped up in the hospital bed
arm in a sling
face pale
a purple bruise across her forehead.

It's silly, really," she tells me,
"If I were a decade younger
they'd set the bone
and send me home.
Instead..." she shrugs, then winces.

"These tests," she rolls her eyes.

Her son
my former husband
sits across the bed
holds her hand.
He holds my eyes with his,
begging me to keep quiet.

He told me earlier
about the blackout
the loss of control
the Toyota fender crushed
against the wrought iron railing
car horn blaring
and,
thank God,
no pedestrians.

I look away.
His need to keep secrets
was a sticking point
in our marriage,
eventually
a breaking point.
I need honesty.

But this is between them.
I kiss Ruth's papery cheek,
pat her good arm.
"Get well," I say, ease out the door,
immersed in the bustle of the hospital
as I head for the exit.

The Reverend

This morning I arrive early.
Sound floats like a ribbon
through the vestry and the lobby.

Outside Thabo's door
I hear the thud
of a body against the wall
rhythmic, violent, heavy
like a sack of dirt.

I knock lightly
"Thabo?"
open the door.

Thabo leans against the wall
eyes closed, face shuttered
arms wrapped around his body
hands in fists.

He pulls away from the wall,
thuds back against it with an impact
that lifts the framed photos of Jesus
children at his feet
shakes the cross on the wall beside it.

His arm lashes out
and he punches the wall
with a force that must crack knuckles, bruise tendons
against the pale wood.
A deep breath, then he groans,
deep, growling,
like an animal in agony.

I move carefully towards him,
lay a hand on his shoulder.
"Thabo, it's Reverend Bob."

His eyes
lost, tormented
flash open, fix on mine
gradually clear
return to the present.

His clenched body sags,
fists release into fingers,
breath slows.

"Are you hurt?"

I take his hand
examine the dark skin
see blooming discolouration
abrasions I hadn't noticed before.

He snatches his hand away
slides down
until he sits on the floor,
slumped against the wall.

His secrets bubble inside him
like lava
ready to erupt.
If only
he could let them out.

"You are suffering," I say
"I can see that.
But you're safe now."

He looks at me,
hesitates
takes a great
heavy breath.

Thabo

Reverend Bob
is kind.
He tries to make me feel
safe.

But these white people
in their soft life
do not understand
what happens
in other places.

In my dreams I see
again
the fires I left
behind

the dangers
in front of me.

I cannot run away
from what
I really am.

But it is too heavy
for me to carry
by myself.

I turn to Reverend Bob
ready to tell
the truth.

Ms Nelson

The heaviness lifts
as I close the door
on the smell of Emergency
head for my car.

I'm meeting Bob at the church
where we're going over
sanctuary cases
looking for a sliver
of opportunity
for a way forward.

Bob has told me
about Thabo's nightmares
about his worry
for the congregation
his fear
that he's being naïve

his need
to face the truth.

I've told him about my discomfort
in defying the law
my need for security
that battles my longing
to fight for justice.

I know
we will be honest
with each other.

Leah

Kevin and I have been invited
for a studio interview
at the network building downtown
to talk about the viral video.

In the walk from the transit station
we turn away from ragged street people
but they see something in our faces
come closer, look us in the eyes,
"Spare some change for breakfast?"
We escape into the coffee shop.

Kevin and I face each other
fortify ourselves
with overpriced foamy coffees
spiced chocolate biscotti
try not to look like suburban kids
just off the SkyTrain.

Kevin's face is pale
small beads of perspiration
form on his forehead.
I lean forward, put my hand on his arm.
"We'll be fine, Kev," I say,
pretending confidence.
"They just want to see
the faces of the creators,
and you know way more
than they do
about social media."

He grips my hand
threads his fingers through mine.
"I know it's not rational," he says
rubbing his thumb
over my hand.
"It's just a blind terror
of public speaking."

I stare at our hands
can't meet his eyes
tell myself
it's fear
that makes him reach out.

KEVIN

She pulls me out of the leather easy chair.
Her hand is warm and strong.
I don't let go
until we reach the massive glass doors.

The lobby is
a buzz of activity
behind more glass.
I glimpse desks, white shirts,
computers, a circle of TV monitors
like a NewsDay episode.

Leah leans in.
"Do you see anyone famous?"
Looking for them
calms me down.

The Personality
meets us at the elevator door,
turns on the charm
with friendly eyes,
praise for our video
for our social commitment.

She leads us to a decorated corner
carpet, backdrop with network logo, couch, easy chair
bright, hot lights
cameras.

A technician clips microphones to our collars,
tells us to talk normally
for a sound check.
I swallow over the fear in my throat.

Leah reaches for my hand again,
grins like a maniac.
"We. Are. Gonna be. Brilliant!"

The sparkle in her eyes
makes me laugh.

She sees inside me.

I think I love this girl.

Thabo

I tell Reverend Bob

Back
on the street in my home
we hide in a back lane
from the police patrol
before full dark.

My street brothers
and I
are shadows in the hot night.
I feel too wasted
to move.

My mind
comes back to me
though I don't want it.

If we cross to the other side
there will be trouble
and shooting
maybe death

like last week.

My belly is full
with hunger and sickness.

Down the road
boys gather around a fire
laugh high, shout loud.

Behind cardboard walls
a mother
sings to her baby.

The voices float to us
on the wind
that smells
of burning rubbish.

The street marks the boundary
between us
and them
between my brothers
and our enemies.
We want revenge,
wait in darkness.

The night smells of coal smoke
and kerosene.
The bricks are rough against our backs.
Police walk by
pick up the street kids
too far gone
to escape.

We cross the street, make no noise,
climb through the warehouse window.
Dira carries the petrol.

We pile broken wood
beside a wall
sprinkle it with petrol.

Mpho flicks a lighter
and when the fire
catches
we disappear like smoke
through the broken window
back to our own place.

From across the street
we watch black clouds that float across
from the warehouse.
Smoke makes it hard to breathe.
We laugh, bump each other's shoulders.
"Whee! we got them now!"

In a window
I see the fire lick
hear screaming filled
with fear, with pain.
The glass cracks
and flames jump
like dancers.

The shadow of a boy
moves across
the orange light.

We look at each other
become quiet
slip away.

Leah

After the interview
still high on adrenaline
we stand in the shadow
of the glittering broadcast tower
repeating our best lines
complimenting each other's shining moments.

Ragged panhandlers
punctuate our walk through downtown
with cries for *"a quarter, a dime, anything helps"*
or rough-lettered cardboard signs
that beg for *anything, anything, please.*

Sometimes people walking by
have to lift their feet
to avoid kicking them.

I think,
Thabo
was one of these,
could be again.

Across the street,
a scruffy, bearded man
sits on the cold pavement outside a café.
A woman steps out the door
coffee in hand,
leans down, passes it to him,
brushes off her camel-hair coat.

His face transforms with a broken-toothed smile

then settles back into a blank stare
at the sidewalk.

He sips the coffee.
His hand shakes.

Thabo

I tell Reverend Bob

After the fire
the police become serious.

The city has had enough of trouble.
Three burned bodies
in a warehouse
is too much for them to ignore.

My brothers
shake their heads.
"It was only to scare them,"
Dira says,
"not to kill them.
They were too stupid
too slow
to run away."

We run, we hide.
The police catch us.
Some are beaten
some shot
some just gone.

After a week
I am the last one
and when I am tired
of running

'M'me moholo
the old woman
who drives around the streets
in her big shiny car
with her big muscled driver

promises
to save me.

The Reverend

When I leave the church
it's after midnight.
Thabo is asleep at last
comforted
       I think
by my reassurance
that he was only desperate
not evil
that what he does next
matters most
that we will not
abandon him
in his hour of need.

I fall into bed
exhausted by the weight
of his memory
and his tears.
Sleep pulls me down.

Thabo

Smoke curls under the crack
of the door,
a pretty grey twist of air,
snaking along the floor.

I lie in the bed
still breathing hard
from another burning dream.
For a minute
I am that boy
in the window
and I think

yes, this is right.
My dream started this fire.
Now is my time
to burn.

The smoke climbs up the curtains
and I hear a roar outside
the door.
I blink awake.

No. I am alive.

I push back the blanket,
pull on clothes,
shoes,
open the door.

I slam it shut on leaping flames,
back away to the window,
crank it open, pull off the screen.

slide through the gap
to the cold air
of the wide world.

The Reverend

The call comes from a parishioner
elderly voice trembling
and urgent.

"Reverend Donaldson,
it's a fire!
The whole church
      on fire,
with smoke everywhere.
      Come quickly."

The cobwebs of sleep
pull slowly off confusion
as I reach for my sweats.
What happened?
An electrical short?
The old furnace exploding?
A candle left burning?

And then it hits me.
Thabo.
My God
My God.
Don't forsake me now.

KEVIN

I'm driving
driven
through the rain-wet streets.
At the back of my head
mumbles the thesis
of my History essay.

I left it too late
my notes a jumble.
I need the late night streets
the mindless spinning of wheels.
The introduction filters slowly
into my brain and I lift my phone
dictate into the speaker.

A text chirps at me as I
reach my thesis.

"U awake?"
It's Leah.
"Yup."
"Fire @ church. Meet there."

I forget my thesis
stomp on the gas.

Street lights illuminate
the empty, wet roads
as dark stores and offices
flit by.
In the distance
the sky glows.

Leah

Dad drives
Brittany rides shotgun
I'm in the back.

We follow the siren wail
then the glow
in the sky.

A media van is parked
behind the fire truck.

As we pull up
Brittany twists over the rear view mirror
checks her make-up
bares her teeth at her reflection
and goes for the TV cameras,
her head high
pretty concern on her face.

I climb out the other side
search the streets
for Thabo.

KEVIN

Emergency crews block the road.
I skid to the curb
leave the door unlocked
sprint through the walkway
to the church on fire.

In the shadow of looming trees,
I spot Leah bent over, searching
in the edges of the light.

In the TV camera spotlight
Brittany sparkles at the reporter.

Paper and embers float on the draft
feather down with the wind
One lands on my shoulder
crumbles to ash as I brush it off.

Brittany

The reporter smiles at me.
I can tell he's glad
I'm ready and articulate
an informed insider.
I turn my head
for the best camera angle.

"We've been supporting Thabo
since he arrived.
He's making great progress
in reading and writing
and learning about Canada.
This fire is terrible
not just for the church
but for him personally.
This is his last safe place
his sanctuary."

"And where is the boy?"
        asks the reporter.

I pause

        suddenly aware
        I have no idea
        if he's even alive.

My mind freezes
as I imagine burning
in those hungry flames.

"We're...searching now.
Excuse me."

I force myself to walk
not run
into the arms of my dad.

KEVIN

Leah is calling Thabo's name
hard to hear
above the crackling flames
and hiss of the hoses.

When I touch her arm
she looks at me with huge eyes.
"The police are watching,
waiting to grab him.
We could lose him."

I'm thinking the same

and then I see him
behind a lamp post
half a block away
looking back at the fire.

"There!" I whisper to Leah.

We scan for cops
move in his direction
slowly
so no one notices

But as we walk
a grey car pulls up
between us and him.
The trunk lid opens
we hear a sharp cry

and Thabo disappears
into the car.

It speeds away
into the night.

Brittany

Dad holds me tight.
I cry in his arms,
afraid of the fire,
afraid
that Thabo has been burned to death

afraid that I won't have any
positive, confident
sound bites
for the reporters.

What have I done?
What can I do?

Suddenly everything
tilts.

I need Kevin.

The Reverend

Police pull me back.

Charred hymn book pages
flutter around us
like pigeon wings.

"There's someone in there,"
I tell them.
"You have to get him out."
They pat my arm.
 "We're doing everything we can, sir.
They're searching now."

The ceiling collapses
crackling.
The rafters explode into noisy flame.

My voice joins
those of the crowd
in a cry that rises
with the whoosh of wind
to the midnight sky.

Ms Nelson

As I pull up to the church
I see the Reverend first

in sweatpants, sweater,
untied hiking boots
hair springing
like a cartoon.

Firefighters hold him back
from the flames,
let him go
when he slumps.

I hurry up beside him,
tuck my arm under his.
He runs a hand
over his face.

"No sign of Thabo.
They aren't sure where it started,
but someone
found a gas can
in the bushes."

I pull back in shock.
"Arson?"

He nods.
"Or attempted murder."

Leah

As the car slips away
we both start running
as if we can catch it.

"No," says Kevin.
"My car, here!"
It's tucked against the hedge.

In the distance
tail lights glow like red eyes,
turn onto the main street.

"There!"
I yell
loud enough to crack windows.
"Go left! They're heading
for the freeway."

"Cops?" Kevin asks.

They didn't look like uniforms.
The car is too old for police
and they bundled him in
like old rags,

like baggage.

It must be
the people smugglers.

Brittany

As I look out
from the circle of Dad's arms
I see Kevin's car
disappear around the corner.
Leah's gone too.

WTF?

Part 4

KEVIN

I try to be subtle
keep back
don't accelerate
or gun the engine too loud.

Leah keeps her eyes
on the car ahead.
When they hit the freeway
we drop back.
The Maps app on my phone
tracks us
along the yellow line on the screen.

I remember all the cop shows I've watched,
move up, fall back.
Even this late
there's lots of traffic.

My phone flashes
"low battery."

Leah stares straight ahead.

Thabo

My shoulders burn
arms twisted behind my back
stuck together with stretchy tape.

I breathe dust
smell potatoes
through the cloth bag
over my head.

I hear words,
African voices

not enough
to understand.

Ms Nelson

The flames have withered
under the hiss of water.
The firefighters work their way gingerly
into the charred timbers
checking for hot spots.

I face Bob
see the twisted torment in his face.
I shake his arm.
"We don't know he was in there."

His eyes lock with mine.
"He shouldn't have been left alone.
He has demons."

"And we'll deal with them
when we find him"
I say

He slumps to the curb
head in his hands
ashes settling over him
like snow.

In the blackened skeleton of the church
something falls,
stirs a whirlwind
of sparks.

Thabo

to breathe
is difficult
through the cloth
over my face

my arms are on fire

I smell sweat
something sour
something burning
in the engine.

I lie still.
I know from before
that if I move
pain will follow.

I listen hard.
The music
of my own language
comes through
the cloth over my ears.

They are not police

but I am deep
in trouble.

This soft Canadian life
falls off
like a shell or a snake skin.

I had good reason
to be afraid.

Leah

I text Brittany
as we leave the highway.

We trail behind,
more visible in the empty roads.
We're past the industrial subdivisions,
deep into farmland.
I'm down to one bar
of cell reception.

A waft of manure drifts into the car,
"eau de country," my family calls it
when we pass the farmbelt
on our vacation trips to interior lakes.

Tonight
it's the breath
of a foreign world.

Kevin grips the wheel
focuses on the ribbon of road ahead
the narrow beam of light
the red dots of tail lights in the distance.

We're way out of our comfort zone.

Brittany

Ms Nelson and Reverend Bob
look like that old farmer couple
in the painting
except they don't have the pitchfork.

They don't know.
They think Thabo's dead.

Grief runs off them like water
into the gutter.

For a second
before I go over

I hold the power of my knowledge
like a diamond
in my fist.

I shake it off.
I'm not like that.

KEVIN

We lose them in the dark farmlands
turn left, left again
think we've passed them,
driving in circles around these stinky fields.

Suddenly they are a country block behind us
the only other vehicle in the darkness.

I pull to the edge of the road.

The car slows down
checking us out.

Leah

Kevin turns to me,
pulls me into his arms
breathes into my neck.
The car slides by like a shadow.
Our hearts thunder against each other.

"We're okay. They're gone," he whispers.

A teenage couple making out
Good disguise.
We pull apart,
look away.

Ahead, the headlights turn
down a long drive.
They've arrived
somewhere.

I text my sister.
No reception.

"Where's your phone?"

"Out of battery.
No charger."

We stare at each other.
It's up to us now.

I reach for the door handle.
The overhead light flashes on
warning signal rings.
Kevin snatches out the keys,
hits the light.

We step out of the car
shut the doors
breathe deep.

Thabo

My throat is full of dust.
I have to stay calm
or I'll choke.

The motor stops.
I roll.

Through the cloth
I see light
feel cool air
as the lid opens.

They pull me by my arms
out of the car.
I crack my leg against
something hard.
　　　"Ahh!" I cry.

A hand slaps me.
My head rings.
I stay quiet.

Hands haul me up and out
over a broad shoulder,
my voice groaning,
my head bouncing.

I am carried into a building
through a doorway
up stairs

my breath leaves my body
when I land
hard
on the floor.

I fight to pull it back.

Leah

We stare across the dark, ploughed field.
A windbreak of close poplar trees hides
a blue house
the car at the end of the long driveway.

It's so quiet
I can hear our breathing,
above us a starry velvet sky.
Far away,
a dog barks.

We are in the flat bottom
of the valley
contained on this side by looming shadows
of rocky hills.
A pungent wind breathes across the field.

Kevin whispers,
though we don't have to
yet.
"We need a plan."

I nod, look at his eyes.
"Find a hiding place.
Wait.
Watch.
Listen."

KEVIN

I stumble
over clods of earth
try not to cry out.
It's harder than I imagine
hiking through the ploughed field.

Leah forges ahead
towards the house
while I swallow my curses
get up
charge after her.

She stops
looks back.
Her eyes are scared
but she's ready to move forward.

As I catch up
I think

Leah notices
when I'm behind her.

Brittany would have kept going.

The Reverend

I stand up
when the walls fall down.
Miranda stands beside me.

Brittany walks over,
an odd light in her eyes
or maybe it's the reflection
of the fire.

We both stagger
at the news that Thabo is alive
taken by strangers
somewhere
up the valley.

We consider our options.
If we call the police
and they rescue Thabo
will they deport him?

His confession simmers within me.
What sanctuary can he find
now?

Ms Nelson

Thabo's safety is the priority

But all we have
is a set of tail lights
and a text to Brittany
from up the valley
somewhere.

Nothing since.

Can we do this?
Ignore the rules?
Work outside the law?

I grip Bob's arm
as I consider

the consequences
intended
and unintended.

He turns to me
as if to speak
shakes his head.

There is no easy
answer.

KEVIN

The house
is faded blue,
two storeys
with two gabled windows
a covered porch in front
a steep, narrow roof
in front of the upper windows.

It looks like it was lifted
from down the street
in my suburban city

plunked down
in the middle of a farmer's field
left to sag for ten years.

Off to the side
is a free-standing carport,
open on one side
a vine-covered lattice on the other.

We work our way
down the drive
towards the house
tuck in
among the poplars.

It feels like we're sneaking into a neighbour's yard
for a Hallowe'en prank.
How can anything so ordinary
be so evil?

But there's the pounding of my heart
the adrenaline sparking in my veins.

Leah trips over a branch.
Her muffled "oof"
echoes in the loud silence.
We creep closer.

The windows
are dark.
We know
Thabo must be in there.

Leah

We stand in the shadow
of the poplars.
My lungs ache with the urge to gasp
but the need for quiet
keeps my breath shallow.
My heart is loud in my ears.

Kevin leans against me
breathes in my ear,
"Upstairs window."

I look up.
One gabled window
is lit from behind.
Dark figures toss in something large.

The light disappears.

I turn to Kevin,
so close I can feel his breath
on my cheek.

KEVIN

Leah's eyes are wide
with horror and excitement
hope and fear.
She looks like I feel.

We survey the dark house
The carport is separate but close

a small gap
between its roof
and the house.

The wooden lattice
that forms one carport wall
looks old,
overgrown.

"There!" she whispers. "We can get up on the roof,
get him down that way."

My eyes follow her pointing finger.
"What if we get caught,
and make things worse?"

We push back between the poplars
to breathe and plan.

Brittany

It's way after midnight
and the TV crews have gone
but the online world
is awake.

I post photos of the fire
do a few more selfies
pick the one
that shows to advantage
my cheekbones
and eyelashes
smouldering ruins in the background.

I Snapchat my friends
Tweet my networks
Instagram my circle,
who I know will share,
update the Facebook page
tell the world
Thabo's missing
after the fire
maybe kidnapped by child traffickers.

We need to get the word out.

I change my profile picture
#GirlOnFire.

Ms Nelson

We page through Bob's smart phone
fumbling with touch screens
sudden ad downloads.
"I saw it there," he says,
"when I finally looked at my phone.
Kevin sent me his location."

At last the screen comes up
They're near Harrison Hot Springs,
a resort town
surrounded by mountains,
a last transmission
before the connection died.

We look at each other.
Police have told us
they didn't take Thabo.
If they find him
he'll be arrested,
deported.

But there's really no choice.
They could all be in mortal danger.

We call over the officer in charge.

KEVIN

Are we really planning this?
A break-out?
Wouldn't it be better
to call the police
let them deal with it?
What if they have guns?

But Leah is crackling
with energy and reasons.
They'll be gone if we leave.
Thabo will be deported
if the police come.

I raise my eyebrows.
Better deported
than dead.

"Up the vines,
over the roof
jump the gap,
climb through the window,"
she whispers, urgent.
"We can do this--
save him."

Leah seems totally sure
of herself
and her plan.

She hugs me, holds my face in her hands.
"Please, Kevin."

I lean down
kiss her mouth

feel electricity.

"Yes," I say, "yes."

The Reverend

Handing over responsibility
leaves relief
and guilt.

Miranda catches my eye.
"We had to do it,"
she says.
"Now if only the kids will be sensible
until the police can take over."

Thabo

It's quiet and dark.
My breathing slows

I make the panic go away.

Around me I hear
whimpers and moaning.
Something bumps my leg
and I realise
I'm not alone.

Leah

Hard to think straight
with my lips tingling.
My heart is pounding
but not from fear.

KEVIN

Now is not the time.

But I look deep in her eyes
let my hand
stroke her face
let her know

this time
I'm not pretending.

For a long moment
we look at each other

before we turn back to the house.

Thabo

Seems like forever
I've been in this bag.
I breathe slow
so I can hear.
The one beside me cries.

I've been in danger before.
I know I cannot let my fear
take me over.

I push my head against the carpet,
pull back,
pull my head free
from the cloth bag

and breathe clear air.
For a minute it's all I can do.

I look around me
arms taped behind my back
feet taped together too.

It's dark
but by the light under the door
I see two other shapes.
One moves, moans.
The other is still.

Through the window
across the room
stars shine.

Was it only today
I ran from fire
in the church?

Or was it long ago,
into a hot Jo'burg night
from a warehouse room
from heavy footsteps on the stairs?

I escaped through windows before.

My arms pull against the stretchy tape.
I need something sharp.

Leah

We crouch together in the shadows
watching for a chance.

The front door bangs open
a man steps through,
cigarette between his fingers
stumps down steps
to the car.

We shrink back between the trees
my heart thunders.
He leans through the open car window,
pulls back with phone in hand,
stands smoking
looks across the yard
at us.

We freeze, hardly breathing.
He flicks the butt
onto the gravel driveway
trudges back to the house.
The door slams.

We breathe again
crawl in the dark
towards the carport.

Please, please
let this work.

Thabo

In the little light
from the hallway
I see in the carpet
a grate, small, metal, with an edge.

Kea leboha, *thank you!*

I twist over to it,
move like a snake,
with fingertips behind my back
work the frame
out of the floor
turn it sideways
rub my arms
against the sharp edge.

The Reverend

I look at the stars
send up a prayer.

Never put much stock
in a God
that would pluck
His favourites
from danger

or not

at a whim

but when I can do nothing more
I surrender
to the yearning spirit.

If ever there was a time
for Divine Intervention
this is it.

Ms Nelson

Bob looks almost saintly
eyes searching the sky.

His rumpled clothing
hiking boots
give him a humble quality.

I worry about the young people
but I'm glad
we're on the same team.

An odd peace descends on me.
I reach out
squeeze his hand.

Brittany

Everyone's talking
about Kevin and Leah
Leah and Kevin.
The fire is old news now.

Police read and reread Leah's text from the valley
my unanswered, annoyed replies.
They want Kevin's license plate number
as if I would know that,
and his cell number
that goes immediately to voicemail.
It's all about them
and Thabo
not dead
but not here.

Ms Nelson and Reverend Bob
their heads together
mutter like conspirators
in the light of the last emergency vehicles.

I'm pissed
they all left me out.
This was my deal.

Only my phone
keeps me connected.

Thabo

I rub my wrists
back and forth
back and forth
against the grate
seems like hours
before the tape is cut enough
to free my hands.

The tape tears my skin
as I peel it from my arms,
my legs
roll my head and shoulders.

I look at the others
both quiet now

I shake my arms and legs
to get the feeling back,
crawl to the window
look out.

KEVIN

We're hidden by old grape vines
leaves rustle
as we climb
move slowly
step carefully up the fragile lattice.

I go first
crouch on the roof
watch the front door
through the gap between us
and the house.
The upper windows are dark.

I reach an arm back
for Leah.

Suddenly a twitch of curtain
a face in shadow
then gone.

Leah

Kevin reaches down for me
hisses
"Someone in the window.
I think it's Thabo."

The Reverend

Brittany's father
bundles her into the car.
She waves brightly from the front seat
with her phone.
Reminds me to pull mine out again.

I have mail.
Parishioners
youth group members
church board,
choir,
all pouring in
sympathy
support
questions.

I show Miranda my screen.
"So many
in our corner,"
I smile at her.

I feel power
grow
from inside.

Thabo

I'm alone again
only me to worry about.

A groan from one of the shapes
on the floor.
I creep towards it
unknot the bag
pull it over the head.

It's a boy
younger than me
more black, more beaten,
face bruised
one eye shut
with dried blood
the other eye wide and scared
mouth taped shut
nostrils wide with the effort
to breathe.
I grab a corner of the silver tape
pull hard
painful but over fast.

He tries to cry out.
I stop it with my hand.
"Shut up or we both die."
His good eye leaks fresh tears.

I wait until he nods
take away my hand
let him breathe, deep and gasping.

I know how that feels.

I put my hand on the back of his neck
feel the shaking in his bones.

"Stay still," I tell him.
"I will let go your hands.
Then we will get away."

He blinks, looks away.
I tell him I am Thabo.
"Joseph," he says.
I tear the tape from his arms.

"Now," I tell him, "we must escape."

He throws his arms around my chest.
"You saved me," he whispers.
"Where is my sister?"

We both look over
at the still, small figure,
hooded and taped,
tossed
in the corner of the room.

Leah

On the carport roof
we pant with effort and nerves.
I watch the upper window,
now in my line of sight.

"Are you sure?" I ask.

"No,
but it was a face,
and it looked like him."

We stare at the window
willing Thabo to appear

decide to wait and watch
before we move again.

Ms Nelson

When we call the police
for an update
the response is cool.
"We'll inform you
when there is something
to report."

Our civil disobedience
has left them
holding a grudge.

I'm desperate to know
and so is Bob.
I look at him
raise my eyebrows
cock my head.

He nods and smiles.
"Shall we?
My car is here.
I have the location."

I nod. "Let's go."

We leave the church
still smoking
behind us.

Thabo

When I pull the bag away
the head rolls back
eyes closed
arms floppy.
This one is small.
Her skin is like a baby's.
The tape leaves
raw patches
on her lips
when I pull it off.
She is light brown, dressed in rags.

The boy gathers her in his arms.
"Palesa," he whispers in her ear,
"My little sister."

I tell Joseph
I think she is dead.

In my old life I would leave her
save myself.

But he won't let go.
Her mouth opens
sucks in a breath
her eyes blink.

I sit back on my heels.

Now
we must carry each other.

KEVIN

We see nothing more
but we have to do something.
Asphalt shingles crunch
as we creep across the roof.

Between the garage
and the house
we look across
the yawning gap.

Thabo

Now we are three
small girl,
bleeding, crying brother,
me.

I could run away so fast
myself
but they are helpless.

"Come to the window.
Keep down."
They do what I tell them.

I look out
to find escape
fall back with surprise.
when I see
on the roof across from us

Leah.

Leah

I look down.
Not so far across
but a fall here
could kill me.

I've jumped this distance before
to make a base.
It's all a matter of confidence.

Suddenly
I look up
see a face in the window.
Our eyes connect
He disappears.

Thabo.

The Reverend

I've never bothered
with the map device
on my phone.
Miranda is a whiz.

At this hour of the night
traffic is light.
We talk as we drive
childhood
her marriage
my lost love

and I tell Miranda
Thabo's story.
She listens without speaking
responds as I thought she would.
"He did what was necessary
to survive in his world."

We look at each other
know
we're on the same page.

The conversation
feels like it's just beginning.

Miles fly past.

Ms Nelson

A cowboy turned minister
preaching in the suburbs of Vancouver.

And Thabo
from a burning warehouse in South Africa
to a church in Canada.

Life takes us in strange directions.

Brittany

I'm answering as many posts
as I can
switching between apps.

I look up.

> Dad is waiting by the car.
> He wants to go

but I have to finish
this one.
#child trafficking
#savethabonow

Everyone's reading me.
It's all so

dramatic.

KEVIN

Leah whirls around
grabs my shirt
I hold her
tight against me.

"He's there," she whispers.
"He's moving.
We can do this!"

Thabo

I open the window
kick out the screen
catch it before it falls.

"Come!" I whisper to the others
boost them out on the steep roof.
The girl tries to cry
and I pull her back to me by her dress
cover her mouth with my hand.
"No! No noise!"

Her eyes are big with fear
but she is quiet.

Leah

I don't understand.
Another boy
not Thabo
and a little girl
on the roof.

At last
Thabo appears
in the window
climbs out
beside them.

Halfway across the roof
the girl's shoe falls off
rumbles down the shingles
sails off the edge
thuds on the porch steps.

A yard light flashes on
and the three are lit
like moths before a light bulb.

Thabo

In the house
thundering footsteps
up the stairs.
They have heard us,
turned on the light.

"Tsamaea! Go! Qhomela! Jump!"
I yell
no need for quiet now.

I push Palesa towards Joseph
who lifts her up
tosses her little body
across the open space
towards Leah's open arms.

KEVIN

Voices inside the house
a burst of light into the room
Leah leans to catch the little girl
teeters on the roof edge
and I snatch her jacket
just in time
pull her back
the girl in her arms.

Men are shouting
One waves out the window
calling us back.
I almost laugh.

"Come on!" I yell
and Thabo and the boy fly over the gap
land hard.

I lead them at a run
to the lattice.

Behind us a shout.
A spurt of terror
speeds us across the roof.

Leah

We scramble to the lattice
caught in the spotlight,
reach for vines
swing over the edge.

The little girl stays close
between me
and the other boy.
"Etsa kapele, aussi!" he calls,
scurries down like a spider,
the girl behind him.

It's like a flying dream
we move so fast
flowing down the vines
like water
not noticing scratching leaves
broken slats.

As we reach the ground
the door to the house slaps open
a man stands in the doorway
a rifle in his hands.

"A gun!" I gasp
and as we race for the trees
he raises it to his shoulder.

I'm last into the windbreak
and as I dive forward between the tree trunks
I hear a pop, a roar
in my right leg a knife of pain.

I scream
Kevin whirls towards me
but my leg still works.

"Go!" I shout at the others.

We stumble in the dark
through the ploughed field
tripping over the rough earth.

A beam of light cuts through the dark
makes our flight
a strobe-light dance.

KEVIN

Leah's scream cuts through me.

She's shot,
shot with a gun
shot and bleeding.
In the flashes I see her leg
through her torn jeans
a mess of mud
and blood.

I want to stop
but she's made of iron.

"I'm okay! Go! Go!"

Thabo

Light dark light dark
the flashing torchlight
catches us as we run
another shot
and we fall flat,
kiss the dirt,
try to bury ourselves.

"No!" Kevin shouts.
"Run! Go for the car!"
I see it ahead.

Joseph drags Palesa forward.
Leah limps behind.
I take one hand, Kevin the other.
Together
we make her go faster.

KEVIN

We roll behind the car
gulping, shaking,
and I reach
for the key fob
in my pocket.

Inside
I'm lit with fear
but stronger
a burning anger.

Shoot at me? At us? At Leah?
Just try it.
Just try it.
We'll get you
you bastards.

Another shot kicks up dirt
two metres away.

The Civic chirps
flashes its lights
as the doors unlock.

We swarm into the car
and at last
yelling with
terror and triumph
we pull away
spitting gravel beneath
the wheels,

grip the pavement
shoot off
into the narrow tunnel
of the night road.

In the distance
sirens wail.

Leah

We tear down the narrow straight road,
between shadowy fields

My leg is on fire
pumps thick dark blood
onto the leather upholstery.
I wad tissues into the tear in my jeans
press down
blood bubbles through my fingers.

Thabo is beside me
in the back seat
I reach out
grasp his arm with my free hand.
His face is bruised
lip split, one eye swollen
half shut. He smiles, croaks
"Ho lokile," winces, smiles again.
"We are okay, my friend."

He clamps a hand over my bleeding leg
holds tight
until the pumping slows.
He's done this
before.

In the rearview mirror
Kevin's eyes
intense and dark
catch mine
and hold.

We bump over railway tracks.
My phone chirps to life.

The Reverend

Miranda has directed us
through a maze of dark country roads
to the resort

ringing faintly with old-fashioned dance music
glittering lights reflected
in the still, black lake.

Kevin was near here
last we heard.

We pull into the parking lot
For a few minutes
look out at the dark lake in silence
not sure of our direction,
the only sound
the rasp of our sooty clothes.

Miranda's phone chimes

Thank God
Thank God
It's Leah.

Ms Nelson

I want them to come here
to the light
and the music

but when I hear
of Leah's injury
send them the location
of the valley hospital.

In the quiet car
Bob and I
laugh softly now
with relief.

I lean over the gear shift
slide my arms around his chest
gather him to me
in a hug.

He hugs me back
for a long minute

starts the car
and we head up the valley
towards the hospital.

Brittany

Finally

Leah answers my like
20 texts.

Then my heart explodes.
My little sister
has been shot.

Something else
about rifles, rooftops.
I don't understand her
autocorrected misspellings.

She's near Harrison Lake Resort
the Romance Resort
with Kevin

but I'll let it go
if she just stays alive.

KEVIN

In the seat beside me
another African boy
on his lap a small girl.
His face is a mess, swollen
and bleeding.
The girl has curled herself
into him.

"You okay? *Ho lokile?*
I'm Kevin."

"I, Joseph. This one, Palesa, my sister."

She raises her head at her name
She is tiny
delicate
dark-eyed
a beautiful child.
Her gaze is flat.
I don't think I want to know
the whole story.

"We'll get you some help now," I say

and follow the directions
of the Google Map voice.

Leah

Ms Nelson
sends me the location
of the hospital up the valley
says they'll meet us there.

Brittany has called Kevin's parents
told them he's okay,
that we'll bring him back
to the city with us.

I feel light-headed,
pass my phone to Kevin
lean back
close my eyes.

Brittany

I ride in the back seat
behind Mom and Dad
as they power up the valley highway.

Mom says Leah will be okay
but I have to see for myself

and I can do what I need to
from the car.

I contact the lawyer
to get the wheels moving
send photos, proof
that will make the government
change its mind.

We have to
seize the moment
make sure
they'll pay attention.

Leah

At Emergency
I am bundled out of the car
onto a stretcher.
I lie back
let them roll me
through the glass doors
watch the fluorescent ceiling lights flash by
listen to faraway beeps and voices.
My leg is throbbing
and numb.

Kevin walks beside me
holds my hand
as the light fades.

I sleep
or something like it
and when I wake up
I'm in a hospital room.

My mother reaches over
holds my face
between her palms
looks full into my eyes.
"My precious girl"

then turns to the Emerg doc
for a professional consultation.

Dad pats my shoulder
shaking his head.
Tears run down his cheeks.

Brittany stands
at the foot of my bed.
Her hand strokes my ankle
through the covers.

The Reverend

Turns out
a neighbour called in rifle shots
and screaming.
RCMP caught two men
found blood in the car
in the house
and that's just the beginning.

They tell us this
at Chilliwack Hospital
where ER staff fix up Leah's leg
tell us she'll make a full recovery.

Social Services take custody
of Joseph and Palesa,
no age question there,
and they are whisked away
into treatment rooms.

A young doctor sponges off the blood
closes the cuts
on Thabo's face.

I hold his hand as the needle dips
in and out.
He doesn't flinch.

Brittany

Leah's face
is almost as white
as her sheets
but Mom says her prognosis
is excellent.

Our immigration lawyer
isn't happy
about waking up @ 3 a.m.
I turn on the charm
and he promises
to get the paperwork
under way.

In the waiting room
Kevin looks exhausted
leans against the wall
his eyes closed.

I page through Facebook posts
as the night crawls by.

KEVIN

My whole body aches
after the bruising night.

But the memory
of Leah's scream

seeing blood pour
down her leg

hurts more.

Thabo

The night is lifting
as we come back
to the city.

We go back to my family's house.
I pet the dog
fall into my soft bed

think
maybe
this is the end

or the beginning.

Ms Nelson

The Border Service Agency informs me
as Designated Representative
that Thabo's deportation
has been stayed.
His case will be re-examined
in light
of recent events.

The whole city
media
public
online
is on fire
to protect a victim
of child trafficking.

Chances are
the lawyer says
he'll be allowed
to stay.

His truth
will stay
among us.

The Reverend

In only a week
the world seems to know
almost
everything

sanctuary
arson
refugee children
child trafficking
rescue.

For the first service
after the fire
we hold worship on folding chairs
in the high school cafeteria
full to bursting
with the curious
the proud
the tender-hearted
the righteous.

My sermon is on
"Suffer the little children
to come unto me"
the tenderness
the vulnerability
our sacred duty.

Miranda nods
and smiles
from the front row.

The congregation is rapt

but I'm talking
to her.

Brittany

She's all over the news
IRL and online.
*Ball player, movie maker, top student
humble hero.*

Kevin stands beside her
in every photo
holding her hand.

Not so nervous now
is he?

She smiles at the camera,
shy
kind of cute.

I'm proud

but

a little annoyed.

Ms Nelson

They tell me Thabo will stay in Canada
Humanitarian and Compassionate claim.

But they remind us
this doesn't set
a precedent.

We're not an open door
for any criminal who claims
to be an abandoned child
for any stateless
paper-deprived
vagabond.

Anyone
could take advantage.

Leah

We win this one.
But I wonder
what will happen
next time

to the next
Thabo
or Joseph
or Palesa?

Thabo

They caught the men
but not 'M'me moholo,
the grandmother
who brought me here
left me
tracked me
nearly
killed me.

One day I think
she will come back.
I look over my shoulder
in dark streets
or when I am alone.

My dreams are lighter now.
Sharing my truth
makes it easier to carry.

Sometimes we walk
along the seawall,
look out at the harbour
back to each other.

When I turn away,
Leah and Kevin
look at each other.

Leah

Thabo's face is healing.
He's shaken it off

it seems

laughs in delight
at his escape.

His English is getting better.
"Really, you and Kevin,
you are very brave, like heroes.
I am grateful
to have such beautiful
and courageous
Canadian friends.
Now I have a good life
a very good family."

He told me his story

the fire
the dead boys
the drugs
the desperation.

It seems he has moved on
and our escape in the valley
is just another episode.

But I can't shake it off.

I taste the terror of the scramble
to escape,
teeter again on the edge
of the roof
as I lean out
to catch a flying girl
before Kevin pulls me back

hear the fear in the voice
that is mine and not mine,
feel the fire in my leg, now a white scar.

Now I'm the one
who wakes in the night
with demons.

Sometimes Thabo and I lock eyes
across the table

in our Canadian dining room.
We see the truth in each other.

KEVIN

Brittany says she's good
with Leah and me.
But she acts different now
cold one second
almost flirting the next.

I don't know
if I'll ever
understand.

Ms Nelson

Bob is remarkably
open-minded
about my agnosticism.

Our conversations
over coffee
dinner
wine

breakfast on my balcony

make my life sparkle.

We're not kids anymore.
We have baggage

but we also have joy.

The Reverend

I think I can finally
say goodbye
to the girl who held my heart
for so long.

So many kinds of love.
We should celebrate
all of them.

Miranda is stern,
strong, principled, funny.

She makes me laugh
makes me think
makes me want to move on

make new history.

Thabo

In this clean city,
this tidy country
everything works
most of the time.
Is this for real?

Sometimes I miss
the hot nights
the smell of paraffin
singing in the dark,
the heartbeat of home.
But those memories I will shut away
inside
for secret times.

I can look at Leah
and see them in her knowing.

I will be Canadian now.
The rest
is history.

Brittany

By the time spring
arrives for good

the grass tender green
the bushes bursting
with ridiculous colour

I have put it all behind me.

Just because he's all
lovey-dovey with my sister
doesn't mean
Kevin can't still be my backup.

There's a village in Northern India
hit by an earthquake.

They need me.

Leah

We have a party in the school lounge
to celebrate Thabo's permanent resident status.
Brittany introduces him.
We clap as he climbs the stage
waves and smiles
at students, teachers
parents, church members, media.
Smart phones record it all.

His speech stumbles
but he's come a long way.

*"I want to say
thank you to you all
who welcomed me with your open arms,
who helped me when there was danger
even to them.
So much happened
but it is behind me, in the past.
Here, is a future
I did not believe in
before I came.
Thank you many times.
In my language,* kea leboha haholo."

Applause thunders from the audience.
Global Leadership kids hoot and whistle.
This is their triumph and they drink it in.

Kevin stands warm
beside me. I feel a tingle
where we touch.

From the stage
Brittany watches us.

Kevin reaches for my hand,
whispers in my ear,
"We're all
starting over."
I smile into his eyes.

Whatever went before

now
it feels like happiness.

Acknowledgements

This novel has been a long time in the making and I have had much help and encouragement along the way.

The Reverend Maggie Watts-Hammond enlightened me about issues around church sanctuary.

Friend and fellow writer Kevin Harkness provided plenty of nudges to keep going as well as lively conversations and insightful feedback on many iterations of the story.

My editor, Alison Acheson, supplied the right balance of enthusiasm, challenge and a dedication to the right word, not the almost-right word.

Maureen Brown, and Susan, Debbie and Joan Phillips offered much needed enthusiasm, belief and exclamation marks.

James and Lucy kept me up to date with life and language in the younger worlds.

Ted was a rock of conviction through the darker days of creation.

Finally, thanks to my students, who have provided me with a lifetime of warm, compelling, funny and heartbreaking stories.

About the Author

Wendy Phillips' first novel, *Fishtailing*, won several awards, including the Governor General's Literary Award for Children's Writing and the Moonbeam Award for Innovative Storytelling.

She began writing at age 11, inventing wilderness adventures while hiking in the sagebrush hills around Kamloops. An enduring love of words took her through a journalism degree from Carleton University, volunteer teaching in Lesotho, and freelance writing in Zimbabwe. Returning to the West Coast, she worked as a bookbinder, a high school English teacher and a librarian.

Now Wendy lives on beautiful Gabriola Island, writing full time, reading just about anything, and celebrating the possibilities of words, wood, ocean, and music.

For more about her writing, see Wendy's blog at:
www.writingwendy.com.

Printed by Imprimerie Gauvin
Gatineau, Québec